# "War of the Worlds"

# BATTLE FOR EARTH

## Book Two

## John Pirillo

# Prologue: Invasion

Their machines of war rose like conquering beetles from the shores of the Thames and began firing at once upon the populated areas of the city.

Crews of those stuck on board the ships at harbor strove to turn cannon on them, but most failed to in time.

Merchant ships and military craft were enveloped in a crossfire of immense blasts of heat. The men and women on them did not stand a chance as sails and wood burst into flames, and gun powders ignited. The ships burst apart in flames, their passengers screaming hopelessly in pain and terror as they died from the explosions and heat or sucked down into the freezing waters of the Thames.

The smoke, rack and ruin of the city drove

the population away from the Thames and into the heart of the city.

Brave men and women, gathering pitchfork, butcher knives, rifles and hand guns rushed to the approaching Invaders in an effort to shore up the defenses hastily thrown up by the constables of the city.

But it was useless. The poor constables, valiant and brave as they were, did not stand a chance. Broken, and cast aside like little more than wooden objects, their bodies were torn, shredded, and burning.

The airs of London burned with the stink of death and dying.

The battle seemed never to end and threatened to obliterate all of humanity. But then one day it all turned around and the Invaders fled back into the Thames, vanishing beneath its turbulent waters superheated now by their advanced weapons.

But was it really over? Or were they preparing to come back? Were they going to launch a new and even more devastating attack?

Or worse yet, did they have plans for something for something far more deadly, and unleashed? Even now on its way!

Something, even more sinister than the annihilation of the population.

# Preface

For a long time, humanity appeared as if it would disappear off the face of the planet, the Martian War Machines destroyed anything and everything that moved.

They were ruthless and cruel as no one could ever have imagined in their wildest dreams. Their experimentation on human beings went far beyond any tales of terror from the World Wars of old.

They were a race of cold, calculating beings, whose intellect was so remote from the simplest of human feelings and emotions, that the word compassion, kindness, friendship, love, and sympathy just didn't exist. Or perhaps had been lost and drowned in the mists of time.

Into that world H. G. Wells and Jules Verne forge a friendship that will be tested as no other as they face the War of the Worlds. A war not confined to just space, but also reaches into time and the unexplored regions of our own mind!

# Introduction

*The distance that light travels in one second is 299,792.45 meters, which, if you walked the distance around our planet would take over 7500 times to complete. That's further than we could travel in one lifetime, no, many.*

*But say, for argument's sake, that light does not in fact move at all, but rather our consciousness moves from point one to point b and calls that the distance. If light, in fact, as has been conjectured does not move, but is instead present in all locations at exactly the same place and time, no matter what place and time, then one would never have to travel further than a step to move forward or backward in time, or from one place on the planet to another, or from one planet to another.*

*Light would be like the thread which sews the garment together, so that the collar, the cuff, and the waist all fit properly.*

*Where time fits into this equation is that it is only a frame of reference. That is to say that time itself is nothing more than an illusion, from which intelligent beings create imaginary boundaries to create imaginary movement, where in fact there is none.*

*The reality of time is the same as Light. Light doesn't need to travel, because its end point is also its beginning point. Physical light is the direct manifestation of a Greater Light and not its equivalent.*

*When humanity finally realizes that there is no time and that they are themselves made of Pure Light, then everyone will have available to them all that is, was and will ever be. There will no longer be more wars, famines, disease and struggles between individuals, families, nations and...worlds.*

*There will instead be a brotherhood of man."*

—Jules Verne and H.G. Wells

And so it is, dear souls that I, Jules Verne, once more take charge of the narrative. I fear that if I do not you will gain the advantage of me and rush to the end of this tale before all the characters and situations are unfolded properly, and I should know because I am Jules Verne, Master of the World.

Seeing as I can now from my perspective of time, it has become clear to me that in order for this part of our story to make sense at all, it is necessary to begin with my first meeting with Wells.

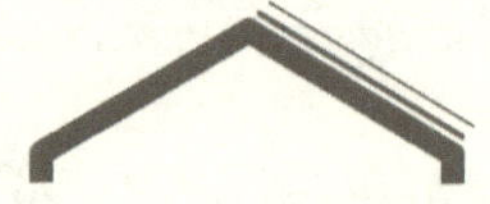

# Herbert George Wells

It all began with meeting Wells, the son of a prominent British Ambassador. While we may have come from quite opposite cultures, our families had a lot in common... the love of family, friendship, and honor.

Wells and I hit it off at once. And what's so marvelous is that we found out we had so many things in common, especially our wonderful imaginations. Those parts of us richly populated our fantasies with Martians, flying ships, invisible men, robotic people who conquered the world, the moon, mysteries and more.

Wells loved the fantastic more than life itself, but his favorite stories borrowed real life adventures of a detective friend we both now have in common...Sherlock Holmes.

Wells and I would sit together imagining ourselves in the shoes of that detective and after reading John Watson's journals about their adventures together, we in turn would take the two detectives in a totally different direction.

We would place them in harm's way using monsters, aliens, and robots. Situations that only a brilliant mind like his and a partner like Watson could possibly deal with. Of course, when we were making those stories up, that pair were already having adventures that made our fantasies seem trivial by comparison.

We even had them take adventures with ourselves. Which looking back on it all now with time that has passed so wonderfully and frighteningly at times, it was certainly a prediction of a friendship to come.

A friendship that the new Holmes eventually with time and careful words and deeds helped to replace the original Sherlock Holmes. But not forget him, just soften the pain over time. A pain that had been created by the murder of Sherlock Holmes by the evil Professor Moriarity.

Yes, we were both blessed with a treasury of imagination that no greedy person could ever steal, or exhaust to conclusion.

We rightly used it on a daily basis, sharing our tales of daring do and wonder. Describing worlds, we'd love to travel to, or that we already had in our rich imaginations.

Neither one of us were attracted to the ladies in our youth, not even as young adults. Don't ask me why. We just weren't wired that way. Maybe it's because we had so much love in our own homes, we never needed to seek it elsewhere.

You see, my dear readers, once we had come to depend on each other in so many ways with our friendship, we found no desire or urgency to extend that need in the feminine direction. This is not to say that we didn't respect the opposite... so called fairer sex, but that we just didn't feel hormonally driven as most other young men of our age were.

But now, in retrospect, as we both look back, I can see how that perhaps may have saved our lives on more than one occasion. For had we been bound to families during those crucial years, we might not have lived long enough to actually grow old and familiar with each other over the decades as older men do.

No Wells and I had a Divine Plan that called for us to be adventurers of the mind, the spirit, and some of the body. And it's that rare combination of spirit and mind, driven by an imagination that allowed us to overcome odds that most other humans in our age group might have caved in to.

Or worse yet...perished horribly.

# The Home of Wells

As you know by now, having already read our first adventure, both of us have been tried and tested many a time. Our lives literally put on the line for each other and those we cherish in our lives, as well as humanity... which while not being quite so dear to our hearts yet remains something dear to us because of our indomitable belief that all beings are in actuality brothers and sisters...if not of the flesh, then at least of spirit.

Wells wrote the first book of this story. With input from myself, of course, even as this will have input from him. No one person can remember everything. Except, perhaps the great detective.

Wells, a bachelor now, as then, never found it in his heart to marry anyone back then. Sometimes I think it is our friendship that has ruined that part for him, for I sense within him a deep satisfaction with our bond, even after all the years of marriage with my beloved Jennifer.

Does this mean that he prefers the company of men over women? I think not. For I have seen in some time streams that he has been a father and doting parent and had a deep and abiding love for his romantic partner.

And I would never exclude him from my love and heart for anything, for even if a man might not love another man in the physical so dearly, he can still love him as dearly in the heart, mind, and spirit, and so it was with Wells and me. And so, it shall ever be, no matter which incarnation we experience across the necklace of time.

But you are probably wondering what happened after the first battle with the Invaders that took place. So forward, or rather backward into what proved to be a very long and painful climb to freedom for many and descent into madness and or death for many others.

I and Wells had many things to ponder after that fateful encounter with the Invaders. Most of it was philosophical at first.

The first question we had to consider and ponder at great length was how we were to unite the remaining survivors of the conflict, to find them and then to heal their suffering souls.

That turned out to be far easier than I would have thought. For news of our victory against the invaders spread like wildfire and even as I had spread notes across France with my wonderful machine where to find me, news spread further and wider through a network that was so hidden and deep that not even the devious Invaders could corrupt or pervert them.

So, on that day that the first survivors found us, I amazed Wells even further. We stood on the porch introducing ourselves to the bedraggled remainders of humanity. Men, young and old, women, children. People of Europe and later the Americas as well.

Wells couldn't understand how so many people could fit into his habitation, which though not tiny, still could not possibility be adequate to the multitudes streaming inside his home. I took him aside when time allowed explaining that I had developed a way of shielding his home from the Invaders' probes, as well as a unique conduit to our sanctuary.

The shielding was a magnificent and brilliant combination of ideas spawned by Madame Curie and Sir Nikola Tesla, with a helpful nudge by myself and a buddy I had met at the Louvre, Albert Einstein.

Al was leading the resistance in Germany, as Tesla was in Czechoslovakia and Madame Curie in Russia.

"That's fantastic," he said in awe.

I faced him squarely. "Oh, there's so much more than that, Mon Ami," I told him.

"What the bloody hell do you mean, Jules? He asked, suddenly a bit nervous about what I might be alluding to.

I smiled.

He hated when I did that instead of answering.

"What?" He demanded.

I smiled yet again.

# Secret Passage

I led him to the back of the home where the people were going, led by several assistants I had stationed in strategic positions throughout the home. As Wells and I neared the kitchen, Hans, a rather large and intimidating Swiss stepped into view and gestured towards the Kitchen Pantry. I smiled. "Hans, this is my best friend Wells, and this is his house, so whatever is good for me is also good for him."

Hans smiled, revealing one exceptionally large gold tooth that sparkled brightly. "Gut to see you, Mister Wells, Jules speaks highly of you. I hope someday to be half as good a writer and visionary as you."

"What is your full name?" Wells asked, shaking hands. "Olaf Hans Stapledon." He replied, smiling even wider.

I grinned, knowing they would hit it off. Olaf had already confided in me an idea that would take the invasion in yet another direction fictionally and was excited when I gave him my blessings to do so.

He opened the Pantry Door. Wells gasped, it was not full of food at all, but a brightly lit tunnel filled with hovering balls of light that floated near the ceiling and lit a path of wood and straw towards a distant dark area.

"This way, Wells." I told him and led him down the tunnel.

Wells reached out to touch the walls, and then recoiled at the touch. "It's..."

# Beneath the North Pole

"Weird. I know." I answered. "You see, the look of everything is totally an illusion to help those who are ignorant and uninformed about the process so they can keep their sanity."

Wells looked at me with a question on his lips. "How is that possible?"

"Wells, remember our theory that we came up with about time and light?"

"Yes." He replied

"It's true."

Wells gasped, sagging against me for a moment for support.

"You alright?"

He straightened, gathering his inner strength about him once more. "I never in my wildest dreams thought we could ever actually make it a reality."

"Reality begins with the vision." I explained with the hint of a smile on my lips. "And then is made concrete by a scrupulous and methodical engineer with the help of many, many friends."

"How far are we beneath my home?"

"Not how far below, but how far away?" I corrected.

He looked at me.

"At this very moment we are entering the deepest and longest glacier at the North Pole."

Wells gasped and then he gasped again as we stepped from the tunnel into a vast chamber filled with ice sculptures and gleaming walls of thick blue ice. "It's..."

"Beautiful. Marvelous. Spectacular. Incredible!" I stated and then added, "Indeed, my dear friend, and without the ignition of our friendship and united minds, and the help of these..."

I led him forwards onto a platform that overlooked a vast hall beneath. As we stepped into view, it became clamorous with the sound of applause. Wells looked down and saw thousands of humans gathered there. As if they had read my mind, they all came to a complete stop in their activities and turned to look up.

Wells tensed.

# Community

I could see terror in his eyes. He turned to look at me, suddenly afraid I wasn't what I appeared to be. He reached for the weapon he kept concealed in his jacket.

I caught his hand.

"Trust me!"

Then the room below exploded into cheers and a thunderclap of clapping hands.

I guided Wells back to the railing. He looked down at the faces all looking up at him and me, smiling, waving, and cheering.

I felt my heat swell with pride. I now had my best friend and my newfound friends together at last.

"I give you our community, Wells. A brotherhood of man that knows no language, no faith, no ideology. We are united under one purpose and one alone, to defeat the Invaders and to restore our world, not just as it was, but to something infinitely greater and divinely peaceful."

I could see that Wells was truly stunned by what he was seeing and had seen. It had finally registered on his soul that his old world was gone now forever and that he faced a brave new world. One he had to embrace...or run from.

Which would he do?

I said nothing as Wells continued to stare, his face filled with one emotion after another as his thoughts flew from flight to safety, to a new world of friends. A world rich with hope and possibilities.

He turned to look at me. Tears were forming in his eyes.

"I don't know if I'm truly worthy of this, Jules," he told me.

I embraced him and held him close, allowing his tears to spill forth freely.

We had both been through so much. Hope stripped. Bodies tortured. Emotions torn aside and tattered. I could relate to my friend's emotions so deeply that I wept as well.

Those below must have sensed what was going on, because they fell into utter silence, waiting to see the outcome.

I trusted my heart. My Wells.

He finally gently pushed away from me, dabbed at his eyes with his handkerchief in a proper manner, sniffed several times, then leaned over the railing and shouted: "MY FRIENDS! VIVA EARTH!"

Below the community of souls as one shouted back, "VIVA EARTH!"

I swear there wasn't a dry eye down there for hours afterwards, but for now let me dwell on what I saw and experienced.

Wells waved to those below, his usually solemn face broken by a grin which threatened to split his face apart. I watched as others below waved back, also grinning and smiling and like Wells continuously wiping at the tears on their faces.

"I think I might learn to like it here." Wells said with great enthusiasm, half way choked by sobs of relief, sobs of pain, sobs of frustration and all the numerous emotions that had been building up in my friend for such a long time now.

I put my arm about his shoulder and squeezed tightly.

"This is my home," he told me. "I can feel it with every inch of my fiber."

"I'm glad." I answered. "Because the way things are going, we'll probably be spending more time here, than at our homes."

Wells looked at Jules. "You think it's going to get worse?"

"Until we discover where the Invaders keep their nest?" He amended.

I gave him a solemn look, which must have puzzled him greatly, as I rarely frown. "Yes. I do."

Wells gave me one of those piercing I-can-see-through-you looks, and then nodded. "Fine. As long as we don't forget about our families."

I pointed to those assembled below. "These are our family now, but..."

At Wells stare, I smiled. "I guarantee you neither I nor anyone else here will rest until all our families are found and rescued, or..."

The way I paused at the end caused Wells to shudder with a sense of deep and dark foreboding. The journey had only just begun, and he knew it had to be fraught with great danger. It already had been.

I waved to those below and then left the balcony, followed by Wells. Our community was now complete, and I knew my friends below would now work harder than ever to prepare.

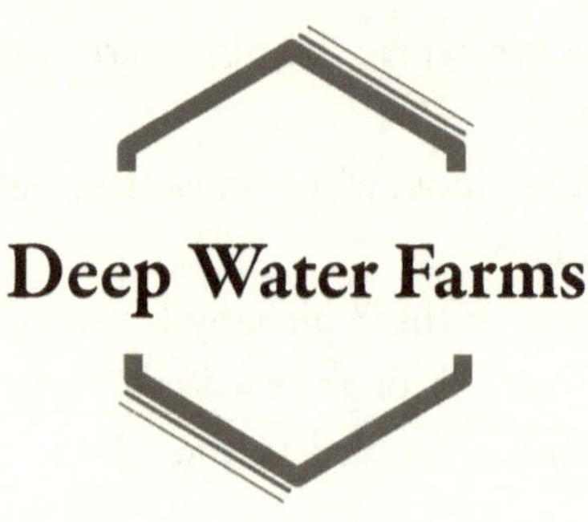

# Deep Water Farms

"Now, we will go to the Command."

"Command?"

"But of course. No war is ever won without a central command. And since all the armies of our world have fallen to the Invaders, we, we... dear Wells... we are the Command."

I led him down a spiraling staircase, deeper into the iceberg. We walked over a long, clear paneled walkway wherein we could see fish life beneath us. Yes, the sea is brimming with life. Below us a sea farm was in the process of being harvested by some of our men. They saw me and waved. I returned their enthusiastic waves with my own.

"These, Wells, are the modern fishermen. They never surface. Always beneath the surface. We have managed to create and build fish farms across the Arctic stretches on both poles. The Invaders may destroy all our land, but they will never touch here."

"How can you be so sure, Jules?" Wells asked me, with a look that said he couldn't believe it.

"Because they can't survive in water, which is why the Invader refused to follow you into the water."

"But it hovered over the water."

"Yes. But briefly. I'm sure their terror was so great that that was why I was able to defeat them so easily."

"But how do you know so much about them, if you've never seen them?"

I grinned like a Cheshire cat, and then touched a finger to his right eyebrow. "Observation, my dear Jules. Observation. Much like a certain detective friend does."

He raised an eyebrow. "Then he's alive?"

"Did you doubt it?" I asked.

He smiled. "The great detective seems to have a knack for avoiding death."

# Command

I gave him a smile, then tapped his arm and nodded ahead. We continued our walk along the corridor until we stepped into a large, spherical chamber. I called it the processing plant, because all our test vehicles were run through every kind of endurance test, we had devised in this space.

Wells and I stopped behind a large, silvered glass window, which had a metallic tint to it. Wells touched it. A slight tingling greeted his finger tip, and he jerked it away. "What's that?" He exclaimed.

"A slight charge. The whole window is nothing more than an elaborate optical illusion; it is actually a very finely tuned force field that keeps everything above the atomic level out, and if need be, even the subatomic level."

Wells frowned. "Subatomic?"

I blew on the fake window and a slight mist covered it. I drew what could have been interpreted as the design of our solar system, but it wasn't. "This is what Tesla and Einstein with the help of Madame Curie have figured out, with a bit of input from yours truly of course."

Wells laughed. "My dear friend, I do believe your ego is threatening to break this glacier."

"Ah, were it only so powerful." I sighed, and then pointed to the sun shape. "The atom, and these planetary shapes, subatomic particles. They are the offshoot of the atom, and just like our sun, the atom flings portions of itself outward to form miniature orbits."

"I see." Wells said, his eyebrows threatening to break off his forehead. "In other words, it's like wheels within wheels."

"Exactly!" I said happily, pounding him enthusiastically on his back. "I knew I did the right thing by showing you this. I think that together we can overcome any kind of physical obstacle these Invaders have thrown against us."

"In time." Wells added.

I sobered at those words. "Sometimes a very long time." I said hesitantly, then my vigor returned, and I smiled again. "But time is on our side. It's our planet. Not theirs. They have to live in their artificial shells to survive, we do not."

Wells frowned at me. "I suspect you have overlooked something, Jules."

I was dismayed at that thought. "Whatever do you mean?"

Wells gestured up and down and all about us. "This whole place is nothing more than a bubble of ice. Ice is solid water. Should it heat up...." He left the meaning dangling dangerously.

"Oh." I answered, sobered by the thought.

"But they have nothing so powerful that could melt the entire glacier," I protested.

"And you know this how?" Wells demanded.

Again, I was at once dismayed by the bluntness of his attack. "Intuition."

"Or ego." Wells said with finality.

At that moment I came closest I have ever come to striking my dearest of friends, but after taking a few breaths, my temper cooled, and reason struck deep into my emotional distress and core again. "Again," I said with a smile. "Once more you reveal why I knew there was every reason to show you all of this now."

Wells touched my arm and said, "I'll help you crew a team to solve this problem we have."

I smiled back. "Then the problem is solved already."

"I wish I were as confident as you," Wells said.

I barked with laughter.

Wells grinned and then he threw hands over his ears as klaxons began to wail very loudly up and down the corridor.

"DANGER! DANGER!" A speaker thundered.

# String Battle Ship

The Klaxons stopped.

Wells looked into the room again and this time his eyes opened as wide as small moons as an immense vehicle began to emerge from its transition through string space.

Yes, with the help of the Asimov-Heinlein engine and the Bradbury fields, we had been able to construct a vehicle at least as powerful as the Invader ships and also capable of hopping, for short distances at this time, through space and time. The engine was the latest iteration of my own ship, The Master of the World, but not quite as artistic, I mused to myself.

The Bradbury fields protected the ship from the pressures of the deep sea we were beneath as well as from the harsh radiation of space. They also protected the ship from loose time streams, saving the ship from Quantum Entanglement that might cause abrasions in the flux of time fields and space time continuums.

I had learned long ago that such abrasions could lead to horrible endings. But that's another story.

Because of the limitations of time travel, such as doppleganging, and paradoxing, we were careful to use time only as a flag point, and never to cross lines in any way that would disrupt them. In fact, if one of our growing fleets of space and time battleships should ever break down in a timeline other than our own, it was to be at once destroyed and everyone in it. Yes. Suicide of sorts, but one guaranteed to save the integrity of all life that God had made in those timelines that were not our own.

For though we now had the power of gods, we were determined not to use the power in a way that harmed life. All of us to the last man and child had firmly decided that mankind must choose a different path that the one it had been on.

Even our weapons were used sparingly, only in self defense. To this point in time, we had held back from attacking the Invaders in their nests. But that could no longer stand. They seemed determined to murder every man, woman, and child of the human population. We could not allow that.

In today's modern society your people might think that's a weakness, but our generation was determined to prove themselves as both physically stronger and morally stronger, rather than using power as a hammer to crush all opposition in the physical as well as the mental. But we, also, were not weak. We would not stand down when we were attacked. We would reply with equal force and in this case...the invasion...greater if possible!

We were assuming the powers of gods but refused to take those powers for granted. Yet still even a kind person sometimes must stand up for themselves and fight back against tyranny.

The battleship transiting from Burroughs-Farmer String Space was a 2nd Class Stringer, armed with heavy duty, rapid firing black hole guns. It could collapse a star into a black hole if necessary. Why such power? Because we could, and because we didn't know for sure if the Invaders couldn't. Perhaps they would rather destroy our world, than see it wrestled back from their foul hands or limbs, whatever they were. We were determined to block such efforts if it came to that.

"Wells, what you see here is the first step of many we will be making over the next years."

"Years!" Wells exclaimed.

I gave my friend a sad look.

"We are few; they are many. Years could be severely understating the battles we will be facing."

"How long have you had this technology?" Wells asked.

I grinned. "Remember two summers ago when I took off to Princeton to do my studies?"

He looked at me for what came next.

"Well, there I met a certain individual. He was a tall, wiry funny man who collected comic books, and books of extraordinary theory. His name was Professor Ackerman. Somehow, we hit it off, and he invited me to his home. It was fabulous. He had every edition of every book, magazine or print that involved theories of any kind that seemed wacky or out of this world."

"Interesting." Wells commented, obviously not impressed yet. "So, he had a lot of science fiction tales. So?"

"Ah, but Mon Ami, even though that appears frivolous, it is but the tip of an iceberg," I explained.

"What iceberg?"

I leaned closer to say, "He was a member of a secret society of Engineers and Scientists. They call themselves the Wings across the World."

"Sounds like my father's Rosicrucian Society." Wells added, his eyebrows furrowing in thought. "Are they then some kind of metaphysical society?"

"Quite the contrary. They are all men of the highest moral fiber who want only one thing."

"Which is?" He asked.

"To save humanity from itself," I replied smugly.

He gave me a startled look. I instantly regretted my tone of voice.

"I'm sorry, Mon Ami; I must sound pathetically overbearing and smug to you."

Wells gave me a sad smile.

"If that were the worst in my life now, it would be a vacation; but it is not."

# Pondering Infinity

No more words crossed between us after that. We both had a lot to think about.

That night we sat in his home, watching the skies from his living room window. We had the balcony doors closed, but a thin gauzy curtain flung over that, so we could still see out, but without anyone about to see us. I was brave. Not stupid.

"Just think of it. Billions of them, extending as far as the eye can see and then beyond." I pointed out.

Wells nodded his head, and then turned to me. "I miss my father."

I SIGHED, BECAUSE I could remember the nights my father had sat me on his lap by the Seine.

We had gazed at the stars for hours, munching on fresh sourdough and sipping cool water from a silver jar.

He would say to me. "Jules, for every spot of light we see in the skies, there is a sun just like ours...maybe bigger, maybe smaller, maybe brighter, maybe a different color..."

"More than Mrs. Bouliare has cats in her house?"

He laughed after I had said that. "Oh, so many more than that."

"Oh!" I had responded, still not comprehending how bit an amount he was referring to.

He ruffled my hair.

"And the wonder of it all...the most magnificent and astounding wonder of it all is that there could be planets orbiting every one of them. Maybe dozens about each."

"More than the marbles I play with, Daddy?" I had asked.

He laughed. "Oh, so much more, my dear son. "

He waved a hand at the stars overhead. Just think of it, try to imagine how much then it becomes possible for there to exist more life out there than here."

"That scares me Daddy," I had replied, feeling suddenly worried.

He kissed my forehead and gave me a hug.

"Oh no, no, no, Jules. I am not trying to frighten you. I want to unravel the splendor of the universe for you so that you do not limit your mind, your imagination."

He gestured at the plants about us.

"If we can have so much life here, just imagine how much more so there could be other life, other life forms out there. Think of the possibilities of life being on just a small percentage of those worlds, and the possibility of life is enormous. There could be millions of inhabited planets out there."

I had clapped my hands with glee. "And Daddy," I would say, "People like us. Would they like to play marbles too?"

He laughed. "Maybe even something more exciting, Jules," he told me. Then his face grew grim for a moment, and he said, "Or something not exciting at all," he had added with a bit of grimness to his voice.

I THINK EVEN THEN HE must have known we would be facing a threat from the stars in the future. Perhaps he like most adults had been forbidden to speak of it for fear of causing a panic, not only in the household, but collectively with our community. We French are a close-knit community, and over our wine and bread, take life quite seriously, just as our dowdy, amiable Italian brethren across the borders do.

Now, in retrospect, I have to wonder if everyone already knew of the war with the Invaders and was just biding their time until it was over... one way or the other. Perhaps they had seen them coming, but as all governments often do in such times, hid the truth from the masses. Well, if so, it worked, but not to our benefit. Civilization was destroyed across our planet. Not in one long, protracted war but in a series of skirmishes where humanity is liquidated in mass and cities cast into piles of rubble and rotting flesh.

All our current comrades were children like us. Forgive me if I put myself as a child, but when the oldest among you are but teenagers, and then one must accept that we are not adults, but children. Children facing an

imponderable future.

There are no adults anymore. They are all gone, unless you count late teens as adults, such as Wells and me. Where the adults had vanished to, no one knew. But it was a mystery I was determined to unravel, even as I had been determined, along with my scientist friends, to find a counter weapon to offset the Invaders.

Wells looked despondent at that moment. I think he felt my own sadness. In many ways it was like we were joined somehow mentally, almost like one soul in two bodies if that were possible. It would explain how I knew where to find him that momentous day I destroyed our first Invader.

Wells had been at the end of his luck, the Invader ship rising to incinerate him, but I had emerged behind the Invader with Master of the World...a magnificent flying machine which can travel through time and space.

I had seen in my heart and mind an image of my embattled friend and rushed to his rescue.

"Wells," I think we need to change the way things have been done on our planet."

"I agree wholeheartedly." He responded at once; his spirits lifted as we moved away from the thoughts of our family. "This whole war between worlds is a bunch of nonsense that should never have happened. If we survive this war, we must construct a society, a government of common good such that we will never be divided again as peoples, or in thought, word, or deed."

"I wonder if that is possible." I replied, having already come to that exact same conclusion.

"But how do we go about changing that?" Wells asked. "We can't legislate morality... the way that a person believes in his soul."

"No. But we can start with the children. Let them be together. All faiths, all colors. Let them grow up together. That will change much that needs to be."

"But that's unheard of!" Wells stuttered.

"New times. New voices," I replied.

"True. But wasn't it just a few years ago. Before we knew of the Invaders that the Germans were attacking the Swiss, the Swiss the Czechs, and the Russians the Chinese, the Japanese the Australians and so on?"

I sighed. "You've made your point, sorry to say. But I still believe it is the young ones who will change everything."

Wells brightened momentarily as a thought of immense import came to him, "Your ships fly through time and space, you say?"

"Not just say. Do!" I replied.

Wells stood up and began pacing. "Then why not use one to go back in time. Stop the Invaders before the war can begin?"

I grinned. "Wells, which would create a paradox. If we knew the future, it would alter it. We must never leave our time ships in any time period, or it would alter everything. We can't even go back to use it to defeat the Invaders."

Wells grimaced. "It would be worth the risk!"

I shook my head. "I spoke with Einstein a long time about that possibility. He conjectures...mind you only a possibility, but a strong one...that if we weren't careful, we could even cause the life of every human being in existence to vanish forever."

"But..." Wells began, his face growing dark with anger.

"There is not but, Mon Ami. There is only what is. And dare we risk humanity's future on a desperate bid to constrain the Invaders? Do we have the right to become that kind of God?"

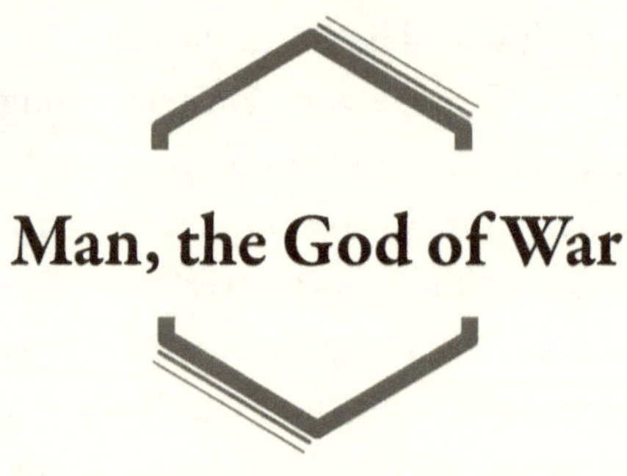

# Man, the God of War

Wells pounded a fist against his nightstand, causing the candle there to shake and almost topple over, spilling hot wax across his lap. Wells scrunched his face in pain for a moment, and then nodded. "But we could try maybe one small thing."

I shook my head. "Sadly, we don't know how that would affect the chain of time events that streams from that one action. You squash a worm yesterday that you didn't before and that worm might have been the meal of a starving bird, which if it hadn't eaten the worm, would not have had a clutch of eggs, which would have hatched into more birds, which would have spread seed across a portion of land that people needed to cultivate. The land might have remained fallow. People might have died that would have lived. Perhaps even you or I would not exist now."

Wells considered that. "But what if we went into an alternate dimension instead, then it wouldn't affect us."

I thought about it. "True, perhaps, but we would have to grow old with the concern in the back of our minds that we could have doomed another world, another life form because of our weakness and poor choices."

"And..." I paused ominously. "What if the changes we precipitated by our selfish actions caused a vehement and violent attack on us in the future by those we had affected."

Wells suddenly understood. "My God! Just such a blundering could have caused our War of the Worlds then."

I shook my head. "Then man has become the god of war and we may be facing a bleak future fighting own selves."

Wells turned his eyes towards me. They were streaming with tears "I am so mad at this, Jules. It's insanity."

I nodded my head and answered him in what I fear did little to uplift his spirits or deny his conjectures, "The more this continues. This so-called war of the worlds, I have to wonder if somehow, we didn't create this war as a result of our meddling with time and space."

It was a gloomy thought. We both felt oppressed by the loss of our loved ones and by the possibilities of suppression by the Invaders that could yet happen. But even with all that we still came out of that night in a happy manner.

Wells sighed, then propped his chin in the cup of his hands on his nightstand. "Somewhere out there. Somewhere, there must be beings that are saner than our own species and the ones attacking."

I put an arm around his shoulder and squeezed. "And someday, I promise you, Mon Ami. I promise you, that you and I...we will...we will find them."

He gazed into my eyes, and I saw for a brief moment my old friend, Wells back again. The one I had grown up with along the fabulous Seine near the Eiffel Tower. A man of hope, vision, and imagination.

He took my hand and shook it.

"My forever friend," he said.

I became teary eyed.

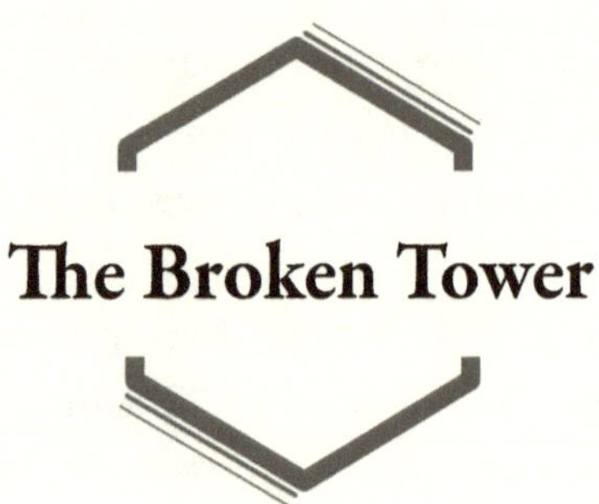

# The Broken Tower

A month later I stood on a lonely pier that overlooked the Seine. The sparkling waters are silvered by a full moon and stand in stark contrast with the remnants of the once proud and majestic Eiffel Tower.

Its top half that had once looked like a mighty sword, piercing the heavens now lay sagged across the bottom half, a sand sculpture made from happier times.

I shifted my feet uneasily, for the Invaders were now coming more into the open. I saw three of their ships hovering near the Eiffel Tower, search lights stabbing right and left beneath them.

I could just imagine the terror and consternation of any who might be alive and sheltering there now. Hard to imagine in some ways, because the adults were all gone, as if vanished from the face of the earth.

The only survivors now were homeless children and starving ones, and usually both at the same time. Wells had been a great boon to me during this last month as we gathered our resources for a push against the Invaders.

Wells had been a firm foundation for me to build our resistance on, even as all our community friends were. We held each other up even during the worst of discoveries, which was when we learned that Beijing had been annihilated. Every single building of that ancient city razed to the ground.

Not a living soul for hundreds of miles about it.

The thought of hundreds of millions of people struck so harshly from existence was a dark one. But it drove us to strive harder; to innovate more; to doggedly continue our search for their nests.

We still had no clue as to the origin of the Invaders, or as to where their nearest bases were, or if they even had any. Perhaps all they did was wander the earth blasting humans and sculpting the cities with their heat rays into molten slag, thus smearing hopes and dreams that once stood as tall and majestic structures built by man across a burnt and desolate landscape.

I don't know. I just know.

For some reason they always left the homes alone. That was something Wells, and I had pondered over, day after day and night after night. Our community continued to grow, but no one coming into it had a clue as to the real and the true motives of our Invaders. We only knew that adults vanished forever, and children seemed to be captured for something, though what was not clear at this point.

Two nights ago, Wells had come up with this grandiose stupid plan.

He had turned to me and said this incredibly horrible thing. Even now in retrospect it makes my whole-body ache, my soul tremble, and my heart stop.

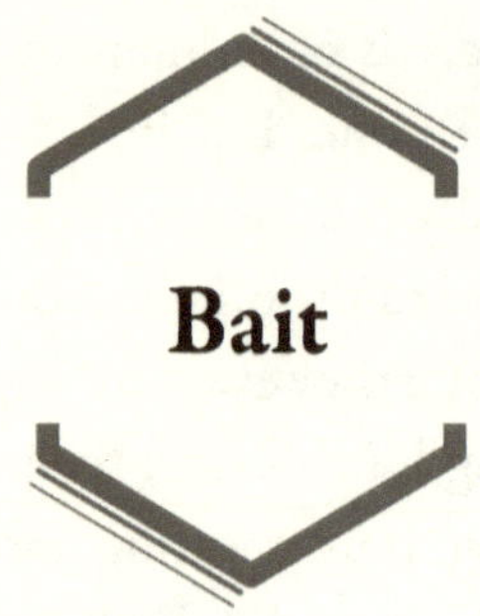

# Bait

"Bait!" Wells snapped.

I gave him a blank look.

"It's this way, Jules," Wells explained as we took a tour of the base hanger, making our way slowly about the new String Battleship in the process of being built there.

"We need to draw them out."

"How?"

He took his hand off the slick metal of the battleship and turned to look me in the face. "Bait."

I got this horrible feeling in my gut that moment. I can still feel it, even now. It was horrible. Like death had just punched me.

"Bait?"

He nodded. "Bait."

"What kind of bait," I asked, dreading his answer. Yet somehow knowing what it would be. Fearing it would be. Praying it would not. But I was to see no relief from my fears.

He sighed, looked down at his feet a moment, and then returned to facing me. "Me. You. Someone who is not afraid."

I was both aghast and horrified.

"Mon Ami!" I exclaimed. "That is total and utter insanity!"

"Has anything else worked up till now?"

I thought back to all the towns and cities now desolate, abandoned, or in ruins that were lost to humanity now; all the parentless children roaming the forests and hills, mountains, and valleys, lonely and hungry. In despair. Hopeless until we found them and brought them to our community.

I finally had to say the word I hated saying. "No."

He grabbed my arm. "Do you honestly think that one of our lives is so precious that it is worth all the lives of so many children?"

I looked away. I could not answer that question safely.

I shook my head instead.

"Jules, they want our children. They kill our adults. Or at least that's what we think they are doing. We don't know."

Wells smashed his hand against the hull of the battleship, winced and then rubbed it. "We can't keep going like this. I don't care how powerful we become. We need to know our enemy to defeat them."

Images of men and women burned to death by the Invaders' war machines instantly lit up my mind with memories I strove with all my heart to bury somewhere, anywhere, but so I could keep my sanity.

I saw my parents as blobs of ash. It made me so horrified and crazy with anger I wanted to rush off and blow every Invader off the planet, even if it meant my dying in the process. But I digress.

Wells knew from the moment he hatched his wild plan that I would be the one volunteering. And I'm sure that was his sole reason for not offering it up before the community. Once I had spoken my intentions, he could not stop me. No one could then.

Despite his immense love and friendship for me, it was not enough to invoke the fear of death to all I love in me. For I have always borne a greater love for humanity than ever just myself. Wells, no less.

No, I could not shirk my duties, nor could I ask any other of our community to do it either.

Wells looked at me to see what my answer would be.

# Paris

So, there I stood on the pier, pondering how to bait the capture as flawlessly as possible, and as all such plans go, it was flawed, because fate had other designs. I heard a scream of despair.

I launched myself from the pier to the walkway and ran towards the houses in April De Mur, the direction of the sound. I had no sooner rounded the corner of the street than I saw an Invader ship hovering over a frightened young girl. She had collapsed into a huddle on the street, her arms over her head, as if that would protect her. I watched in horror as the Invader struck her full force with a blast of energy. But it didn't annihilate her. I noted that its color was a pale green, so I knew from that moment that such rays were harmless to the physical, while not necessarily non-destructive in force. Meaning, this one was non-destructive, but perhaps with a slight retuning could be annihilative.

I dropped behind a porch to watch as the girl was slowly levitated through an opening hatch in the bottom of the Invader ship. A reddish glare emitted from the opening. Strive as I might I could get no view inside without risking myself as well. I was not afraid of dying, but I didn't want it to be a worthless death. I knew I could not fend against such an overwhelming mass of destruction as these ships were without my own vessel.

But I could do one thing, and I did. I hurtled a small lump of goo I always kept at the ready in my right pocket. The goo struck the side of the ship and seemed to quiver a moment before it stabilized. I smiled.

# Base

Our Antarctic Base was frantic with activity when I leaped from my string ship, across the hanger to the entrance to the corridor that led to Command.

I was breathless and looked like I'd seen the devil, which I almost had. Wells was the first to notice me.

He had stepped from the farm room where men and women suited up to harvest our food in the deep waters.

He was always the first. Sometimes I feared he spent every hour seeking me out or fearing for me. I shouldn't have been surprised, as I felt the same for and about him. We were one soul in two bodies, and that would never change.

"You look like hells behind you!" Wells accused.

"It is. And for some children, it's all around." I spat back, still running.

Wells ran after me. "What's going on?"

"I've got a tracer on one of the ships."

We reached Command and ran to the balcony. I smashed the klaxon warning button on the wall. The room below broke into frenzied movement and sound as I stepped to the balcony to look out.

Wells turned the Klaxons off.

Everyone working below and in all the ships turned to look. "Code Retrieve!" I yelled.

Immediately there was a cheer and then an immense sobering because the next steps would decide whether we could finally bring the war to the Invaders or not. "Wells, we must hurry, or a child's life might be in grave danger."

We sped to the hanger bay where my Master of the World hovered on soft rays of stringer energy that glowed in blue and soft tones. I climbed a rope ladder to the hatch and Wells followed. Later on, there would be an automatic ramp and I would reconstruct the ship to a size worthy of its name: The Master of the World.

For the moment though there was only room for two in my ship, but we were working on bigger, just didn't have the resources yet to construct them. Soon. We had communities in Africa working on the steel and softmantium, needed to cure the metal, so it was string space worthy.

I dropped into the command chair and Wells took station at Communications and Weaponry. We had been training with this combination for some weeks now, using remote parts of the Sahara to target practice.

There are now over a dozen String Battleships, but only mine had weaponry, as the rare metal needed for the weaponry was in Russia, and the Siberian area where it was found had been compromised. Until we found another source, we would only be able to build transports. We could go back in time, but the danger and the risk of doing such a thing far outweighed the benefits in my mind.

Or perhaps I wasn't desperate enough yet.

"Tracking on," I said as I palmed a glowing red button. "Ignition," I spat next, striking a cool blue bar that swung back into a recess. I grabbed the steering wheel before me, and we began to arch skywards.

"Blue. Open the roof." Wells said into his communications.

"Opening, Master." A tinny reply blasted over our internal speakers. "Launch when ready."

"Launching." I said, and then pushed the steering wheel forward, while depressing a pedal on the floor with my right foot, and a left one with my other. In moments we were shooting up into the Antarctic night, a burst of green and blue radiance arching behind us, making our string flow look like a Borealis on the horizon. This was something Curie and Tesla had come up with to help cloak our string ships when they flew into the atmosphere.

The Invaders thought it was just a natural display of atmospherics. It wasn't. It was us. Coming for them!

I leveled us off to orbit the Earth and kicked back a moment, studying our position on our screens. "Looks good." I spoke.

Wells nodded. "Communications still crystal. Picking up the signal loud and clear. Should have a fix in five, four, three, two, and one."

Wells growled and punched a button. In the air before us the co-ordinates formed and the outline of a large city. "London." Wells uttered breathlessly.

"Well, Wells, pardon the pun, but it looks like you get to see your home once more."

"If there's anything left of it." Wells replied darkly.

I eased back on the engines and our cockpit shifted earthwards ever so slowly, then I punched our acceleration. We shot towards the ground like a comet from heaven.

# Piccadilly Square, London, England

Piccadilly Square was dark and lonely. Even the few strays that ran across it were gone this night. A lone figure sat against a bench, drinking from a wine glass, singing to himself, until the radiance of an Invader ship caught his attention.

Too slowly, the man staggered to his feet. He held up a Bible and exposed it towards the antenna of the incoming Invader ship. "God forbids you to come here. You have broken His laws. You will be brought to justie for this. I swear this is so in the name of our beloved, Lord God!"

The Invader stopped, and to the man, it seemed as if his words had created the pause, but then the antennas made a thrumming sound and twin rays of massive destruction burst forth, engulfing the man and his Bible. They vanished in an inferno of flames.

The Invader ship remained paused, then slowly glided forth until it neared a huge church front. The pavement in front of the church began to boil as if melting, and then ever so slowly it puckered until a narrow entrance opened in its throat. The Invader ship opened its belly, emitting a garish red light in which the bundle of the girl child was enclosed. The bundle descended into the opening, which slowly began to close up.

"Don't!" I warned Wells as he started to move from the safety of our hiding place, an abandoned carriage turned over on its side. "We know where she is. Now we must see what follows next."

What followed next was not what we expected at all.

The pavement, not even two feet from us began to boil and perk. We backed off, seeking cover. We dropped behind some hedges and peeked through them as the pavement puckered and made an opening. Several moments later the same girl who had descended into the opening in the street began to rise from the new hole.

Wells grabbed my arm. "Impossible!

I said nothing. My mind was tinkering away at a million miles an hour. This was insane, but there was always a method to the madness. When you remove the possible, that leaves only the improbable. In this case we had the impossible, but the possibility was lurking in the shadows behind it.

"Wells, I think they are duplicating us." I whispered; my throat tight with bile. For the girl had risen all the way. Her eyes were towards us, but they were as empty as the paintings on Wells' living room walls, even more so, as no light of awareness hid behind the lens of those eyes.

But then an even stranger thing happened. The eyes began to fill up. No other way to describe it. The empty girl became filled with personality. Her eyes lit up and she smiled, then turned and skipped off down the street, singing a simple lullaby about lost sheep finding their way home.

I felt these horrid shivers go down my spine. This was insidious. What had happened to the real girl? Was she dead, her vital memories shifted to the empty vessel that had just risen from the pavement, or was she somehow still alive and connected?

Wells tightened both hands into fists. I had to hold him down, for at that moment the Invader ship had turned its antenna in our direction. They pulsed with energy for a moment.

Wells and I both held our breaths, expecting the worst, but hoping for the best. Then a rabbit we hadn't seen, hiding beneath some of the rubble, burst from hiding and sprang for new cover away from the hovering War Ship.

Nothing happened. The antenna swung on and abandoned our position. Our lives were spared by a miracle of Mother Nature. So simple as to draw laughter of relief, by one of Earth's humblest little friends...a rabbit. Never again would I eat rabbit. Even if starving.

Slowly, we crawled on our bellies back from the view until we could get behind the building. We then got up and ran as if the devil were behind us because it was. My mind was racing overtime as we dodged in and out of the streets and buildings, heading back to Wells home.

What we had just seen totally changed the entire equation of this invasion. This was not just us against them; it was us against us, or what appeared to be us. "Dear God," to quote Wells, things couldn't possibly have gotten any worse, but they had. How in the world are we expected to spot the traitors in our midst?

"It's gone!" Wells screamed.

I stopped beside Wells and looked where he gestured. Where the young girl had risen from. There was nothing there now. The opening was gone; the puckered earth appeared no different than it had before she had risen.

I blinked my eyes, but nothing changed. There was nothing there. Nothing but a burned-out splotch of earth and smoldering ashes.

The remains of the real girl?

I put a hand on Wells' shoulder. "I'm sorry."

Wells' voice turned cold as ice. "I shall make them pay dearly for this."

"It's only a home, Wells." I encouraged, trying to soften his anger, for fear of him doing something suicidal. "New homes can replace the destroyed ones. Besides, you don't even live in that place anymore"

He looked at me, his eyes smoldering with anger, just like the heat rays of the Invaders seemed to smolder before they fired. "No. You're wrong. There is no replacement. They've taken everything from us and now today we have seen that they mean to take our bodies as well. We shall have nothing left of home, or ourselves. Nothing!"

"But Wells, this is only your English home, you still have the one in Paris." I told him.

Wells hardened further. "True. And you've seen what they did to that home as well. We owe them, Jules. Owe them big time. They are taking away everything that ever had meaning for me and to me. I shall make them pay dearly. This I swear!" He hollered with a force that startled me.

Wells had never been as aggressive as I, and now he was showing terrible signs of distress. Some doctors called that a peculiar name, a mental disease that disfigured the men's souls forever.

I prayed this war wasn't tearing away at his moral compass. For even though I still held an ounce of doubt about the Invaders, yet I hoped, hoped that perhaps there was something we had yet to uncover about them, that would enable us to make friends in the end, or at least understand why they hated us so much.

We heard a humming sound growing louder and closer, so we abandoned our post and hurriedly, but carefully made our way back to the "Master of the World," my string ship.

There would be no final battles this night.

We had come to learn a secret. We had. And were we the better for it?

Perhaps.

Time would tell.

# Paris

It was early August, and the winds were terrible that time of year over the Seine. We watched through the cockpit window as the still standing Eiffel Tower came into view.

"Just look at it, Wells, a symbol for strength. It is still standing, despite all the terrible things that have happened. But no sooner had those words passed my lips than a vast explosion of light enveloped the tower.

I backpedalled on our descent and hovered, watching in horror, hearing Wells begin to weep as the light was swept away to reveal a huge, charred splotch that used to be the base of the Eiffel Tower. Nothing remained of the magnificent structure. Not one piece.

Wells puts a hand on my shoulder then. He

must have felt my grief as much as I had felt his own earlier. "This is too horrible, dear Jules. I am at a loss what to say or think."

I took a deep breath, my eyes searching the horizon for signs of the Invaders. "No Wells, this wasn't a war of the world's event, but an earthlier one."

He looked into my eyes. "You mean!"

"Yes. I think our duplicators are behind this. And if so, that would some of the mystery."

"But not all. Or why they need to be." Wells interrupted. "Their weapons are so powerful, why would they need surrogates? It doesn't make sense. It's impossible!"

"Remember your own words, Wells." I chided him. "When the possible is ruled out, then the impossible remains."

"My God!" He shouted in my ears. "They are too few."

I nodded my head. "Exactly. Too few. They are not a massive, unlimited resource of peoples come to destroy us, but a limited one dependent upon untapped resources to carry out their scourge of a planet."

"How long do you think they've been doing this?" Wells asked somberly.

"Too long." I replied.

"Now that we know what they can do to us, we will be more careful. And if we're careful, perhaps we can turn this tide of battle in our favor forever."

Wells didn't reply, he was watching, as I, as the ground swept away beneath us, and we ascended towards String Space and our home beneath the frozen wastes of the Antarctic vanished from view.

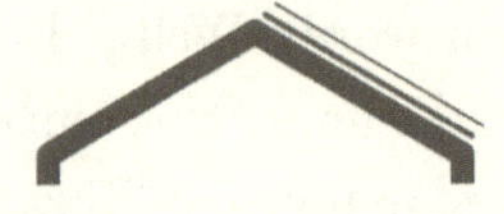

# Homeward Bound

"Where will this all ends?" Wells mused.

"When we utterly destroy these monsters?" I replied with a faint touch of hope.

"Or" Wells added, waiting for the rest of my words.

"Or" I replied.

Or!

And on that unhappy note, we went ahead towards an uncertain future. Yet, a future we had every intention of making safe for humanity.

# Sherlock Holmes

# GEARS OF WAR

# Incident: The Warehouse of Shame

Two sailors, drunk out of their minds, sang a tune completely out of tune, but neither one noticed. They were too busy trying to stay on their feet and make it to the front door of a warehouse with a sign hanging from over its entrance that advertised: Pleasure for the Night, Midnight Angels waiting to make you comfortable.

"I want some of that, I do, Matey," the taller Sailor said, swiping at his beard. "Getting comfortable is something I've been thinking about for months now on that old tub of a ship we sail for a living," he laughed.

The shorter Sailor snickered, and then belched. "Got some the other night and it's the best there is too."

"Here? You never told me about here!" The taller Sailor complained.

"Need to know," the short Sailor said with a sneer.

"And you didn't need to know," they both said together, and then burst into laughter.

Just as they reached several yards of the door, the door exploded off its hinges and burst into flames, then scattered splintered wood and fragments into the two men and across the wharf.

They fell onto their butts, and looked on in surprise as a tall man, wearing a strange mechanical looking trench coat with glowing orange buttons on the inside strode out, carrying two men. One on each shoulder. He turned around and hefted a huge exotic pistol and fired into the warehouse just as a fourth man came running out with a huge, odd sword in his hand that glowed on its hilt and had antenna on its sides.

"Die traitor!" The running man yelled.

The tall man grinned. "Your deduction is premature, old chap!"

Then he fired into the man's chest.

The man got a huge look of surprise on his face. His eyes went wide as small tea cup saucers and then he let out a moan loud enough to wake up the dead and fell face first onto the wharf planking.

The tall man looked at the two sailors as they struggled to their feet.

He took out a business card from his odd suit and handed it to the taller Sailor, "Make sure this man makes it to Scotland Yard and there will be a reward for you. This is your ticket to the reward."

"Who are you, mister?" The shorter sailor asked, eyeing the card over his friends' shoulder.

"Steampunk Holmes!" The tall man said with a grin. He grinned even wider.

"Never heard of you," the taller Sailor said.

"Not matter!" Steampunk said, his smile broadening. "If you haven't, then you soon will. I am famous, you know!"

"No, we don't," the short Sailor said.

Steampunk glanced at both of them. "Just bring this dirt bag to the Yard and collect your reward. Hurry along now and be good lads, will ya?"

He strode off with the two men over his shoulders, and under his breath muttered, "Heathen!"

The two sailors heard the sound of women's voices, and several began streaming out in petticoats, looking frightened.

The taller sailor looked at the fallen man, then at the women.

"I think this fellow isn't going anywhere. What do you think?"

"I think you're right."

The Midnight Angels watched and when they finished, clapped their hands, and ran to the two sailors and hanging onto them like a second skin, hurried them into their den of pleasure.

No sooner did the front door slam shut, and then the fallen man groaned and rolled over. His eyes were swollen shut and he was bleeding from a dozen places on his head. He felt the wounds a moment, groaned even louder, then slowly, slowly, slowly reached to his right boot, which glowed soft blue color. He found a glowing green button and depressed it.

With the end of that motion, he let out one more last gasp of pain and then his body became wrapped in furious green energies.

Captain Bligh, on his way back to his whaling ship, spotted the fallen man and the energies and froze to watch.

The man vanished in a tiny explosion of green flurries of color. When the light cleared all that remained was a pile of clothing and scorched bones.

Captain Blight crossed himself over and over and then hurried to the door of the warehouse, pounded on its door.

"Let me in! You should know what just happened out here, lassies!" He shouted.

The door opened, but before he could say further, five pairs of arms reached out and jerked him inside. The door slammed shut once more.

# Distress and Death

Terry Ackerson chomped on the carrot he had just bought at the local market. He had got a great deal on the last of them. He always did. He made darn sure he was the very last customer. If there was one thing, he was always good at, it was being the last customer.

Roy Bathes, the owner, liked Terry and always sold him whatever remained for a few bits of coin. Saving him having to throw them out and Terry enough money so he could squeeze by on rent again.

As much as he loved carrots though, he longed for the taste of a good slice of bread with marmalade and honey slicked across it. Butter would be an added nicety. But butter was expensive unless you made it yourself. And then you'd have to have milk, and with no cow, you would be forced to pay a pretty penny for that as well.

So, carrots. Not just carrots of course. He would grind them up into a soupy mixture and stir them into a mix of eggs and stale wheat flour he bought at the vendor next to Farmer's Heaven, where he would buy out the eggs left from that morning. No one refrigerated anything. London was usually more than cool enough to keep food items until the end of the day, but not the end of the next day. No one wanted to pay top price for day old anything. So, farmers gave away their products for pennies on the note and purchasers were glad of it. Terry was one of those patrons of the eggs.

Of course, if you were one of the lucky wealthy ones, you could buy one of those new Tesla refrigerators that made noises like some kind of spanked dragon and kept your goods nearly freezing for days and even weeks. But for him, that was just a fanciful dream and nowhere close to the reality of his circumstances.

He had learned by now to make eggs for meals in so many ways that he even thought at times of starting a class to teach a thousand and one ways to make eggs for a meal, but he suspected there were just as many as he who could do the same, so skipped the idea.

Maybe if he hadn't, he wouldn't have been walking home on that fatal night.

"Sir!"

He stopped mid-chomp on his next carrot and twisted about to see who had called upon him.

It was a tall man with piercing eyes. But there was something off about him, though he couldn't put a finger on it. Yet, nothing to be afraid of. He was too poor to be robbed of much more than a few pennies. And he wasn't worth killing, so what did he have to lose by a little kindness? His carrots? He could live without them too. Might be good to take a day or two off anyway. So, he rationalized to himself.

Another mistake.

"Yes?"

The man smiled.

Terry smiled.

This was great. He'd met a smiling stranger. Maybe his luck was going to change.

Then the man pulled a very strange device from inside his jacket. He'd wondered why the fellow's jacket bulged over his right side so much.

"What's that?" He asked, still oblivious to what was going on.

"A thank you present," the man explained.

"For what? All I did was stop and smile."

The man lost his smile. Suddenly, the man didn't look so nice anymore.

The device in the man's hand lit up like it was on fire. It made a strange humming sound. Smoke came out of the sides of it. Steam. Was it some kind of steam weapon? If so, why? All steam could do was...

He didn't get to complete his thought. A burning blaze of brown energies struck him in the chest.

"Dear God!" He managed to gasp and then he collapsed to the pavement.

The stranger bent to look as several carrots spilled from Terry's basket he had been carrying and rolled to the tip of his booted toes. Toes that were in armored boots with strange cylinders and gadgets attached to them.

"Got one!" The stranger yelled.

Two men, dressed like normal Londoners, except for their boots, ran from the nearest alleyway, stooped, and picked up Terry beneath his armpits.

"Thank the Goddess!" The stranger said.

"Thank the Goddess!" The two other men said.

"Hey! You three!"

The three men turned as a constable strode up, looking angry and imposing. He had his nightstick out, ready to clobber anyone who got rowdy. "What's he doing like that?"

The stranger smiled kindly. "A friend. Had too much to drink, I'm afraid."

The constable eyed him and when the stranger didn't flinch beneath his gaze, he nodded and was prepared to leave, when he noticed the man's boots. He quickly glanced and saw the other men's shoes had the same.

"Hey! Who are you guys?" He yelled suspiciously.

"Really, everything is fine, constable," the man insisted, continuing to walk away with the man they had picked up.

The constable saw the burn marks on the man's chest when he walked beneath a Tesla streetlight.

"Hey you three! Put that man down at once!"

The stranger nodded affably. "Sure, no problem. We don't want any problems, constable."

"We got our quota, let him go," the man on the right told the stranger.

"It's not about quotas; it's about war!"

He scowled at the others, and they cowed into submission and helped him lower Terry safely to the pavement. When they finished, they stood back up and slowly reached inside their jackets to pull out their weapons once more.

"That's better," the constable said, walking towards them, thinking they were going to be compliant.

But he was as wrong as Terry had been. They weren't going to be anything that he would like or remember.

They waited until the constable was within a yard of them and turned as one, fanning out as they did so, so that the constable had three of the odd energy weapons aimed at him.

The constable stared in amazement, surprise, and a growing sense that he had bit off more than he could possibly chew.

The weapons looked like pistols, but they had too many barrels and glowing parts. And they had steam rising from tiny smoke stacks on their handles.

""What in God's name are those things you're holding?" The constable demanded.

"Not in God's name, but in the name of the Goddess," the stranger said and then fired.

The energies that blasted the constable were not brown, but a hideous red and green. Smoking as it struck.

The other two men did as well.

The constable didn't just collapse like Terry, instead his entire body burst into flames. The three men hurriedly grabbed Terry again and ran off into the alley.

The constable's body fell to the pavement and continued burning for another few seconds and then it exploded.

# Scotland Yard

atson, Challenger, Conan, and Harry stormed into the building, bundled up against the sudden onslaught of rain that flung itself hard from the skies overhead. No one had expected such a thing. But lots of unexpected things were happening lately.

"It's got to be related to the strangers coming into our world," Harry said without any sense of doubt in his words.

Conan shrugged. "Wet is wet, despite the reasons." Then he slipped off his overcoat and slung it on a coat rack, even as Harry, Challenger and Watson did the same.

"The Inspector's waiting for you gentlemen," Constable Evans said, greeting them with a warm smile.

They followed him through the busy office to the back where the Inspector's office was.

"You're quite busy for a Monday night, Constable Evans."

"You'll see why in a moment," Constable Evans replied mysteriously.

The four men were escorted by Constable Evans into the Inspector's office, where the older man sat behind his desk, shuffling through a stack of reports.

"One, two, three, and four…" He looked up at them as they entered and took seats. "Thanks for coming." He grabbed his pile of reports and shook them at the men. "This is just since an hour ago."

"What in God's name are they for?" Conan asked.

Watson waited for an answer.

Instead, the Inspector nodded to Constable Evans, who went outside, then came back with a loud sounding man following him.

Steampunk Holmes strode into the office, beaming. "It's so good to see all of you again!" He announced and turned to shake the hands of every one of them so vigorously they thought their heads might fall off."

Watson almost didn't do it, but something inside him stopped him when he caught a close look into the duplicate Holmes face. Pride and something else. Something much deeper, more uncertain. A sense of loss, maybe pain.

Watson shook the man's hand, but the duplicate Holmes, Steampunk, didn't let go at first. It was as if he were trying to convince himself that the handshake was real, but when the others looked at him, he finally let go and gave Watson a look begging for forgiveness.

Watson did so, but not openly. He allowed the man to sit next to him.

"Good, let's begin," the Inspector said.

He held up the paperwork again. "I have here thirteen separate reports of citizens encountering strangers with glowing boots and odd weapons who struck down men and women and carried them off."

"That's terrible," Conan said, his eyes looking sad.

"What's more, at least four of our staff...all constables on their beats have been found..."

The Inspector began to choke up. He nodded to Constable Evans, who gestured to the seated men to follow him as he went forth from the office and took a turn from view.

# Unnatural Death

Watson examined the last of the four dead constables as his friends and Constable Evans looked on. All of them seemed frail at that moment, the horror of the remains touching their hearts as well as their stomachs.

Conan nudged Challenger. "I wish we had been warned about this before we ate that meal."

Then he made a gagging sound and rushed from the room.

Challenger looked after his friend. "Poor Conan, a doctor with a weak stomach."

Then he felt his stomach roll over and he ran after Conan, holding a hand over his own mouth to keep the vomit from spewing everywhere.

Watson turned to Harry and Constable Evans. "I'm afraid they have all perished from the same thing."

"Which is?" Constable Evans asked, steeling himself further against the horrors before him. He himself had eaten not that long ago, and while used to worse, he knew the names and faces of these men. His fallen comrades. Jerrod, Harold, Ben, and John.

They all had families and friends in common. They had eaten dinners and drunk together after work at the local pub. They had shared shifts and horrors over the years. But none of them could have expected this to happen. Not to them. Not to anyone.

Watson used his gloved right hand to clasp a surgical plier and stir over a piece of charred bone. "It's most interesting. For a man to burn so thoroughly, he would have had to experience a temperature exceeding that of the surface of

the sun."

Conan and Challenger returned to the room, wiping their mouths with handkerchiefs. They settled about the table, listening to Watson.

"Two thousand degrees Centigrade," Harry explained for Constable Evans sake.

Constable Evans nodded. "Hot enough to bake my bread in and then some, I reckon."

Conan smiled at the comment. "And the whole bakery store as well," he joked.

The men had a laugh, but it was a strained one, speaking poorly of the joke Conan had tried.

"But Watson, we all agreed that these men were incinerated in an unusual manner. Exactly, what were the instruments that caused it to happen?"

"Steam."

"What!" Conan blurted out.

Harry just smiled.

Constable Evans screwed his eyebrows together in thought. "But isn't that impossible? Steam evaporates at anything about a hundred or so degrees temperature, doesn't it?"

Watson nodded, "Depends. If the air is cool when a fire begins, the heat of it will produce steam, just like boiling water does. Like your breath when it's freezing outside. But for steam to have such a powerful effect, the poor men would have to have been struck by immensely powerful streams of superheated steam. Any weapon capable of that would by its extremely hot nature be as likely to kill the person holding it, as the person intended the victim."

"Unless, dear chap," Steampunk Holmes said, as he stepped into view from the doorway where he had been silently standing, listening to his friends.

He stopped next to Watson. He smiled. "Brilliant deduction, but there's more."

Steampunk Holmes slid a hand down his chest and at once one of his pistols sprung up into his hand. He twirled it about and handed it barrel first to Watson.

"Fire it!"

"In here?" Watson exclaimed with horror.

"I merely ask it to prove a theory...or" he smiled, "Disprove and correct one." He finished, giving Watson a scholarly smile.

Watson frowned in annoyance but nodded anyway. He turned and faced a door in the back of the room. "Constable?"

"No problem, Watson. It's double shielded steel, reinforced with concrete. Worst thing that could happen is you would warm it up a mite."

Watson nodded again and depressed the trigger on Steampunk Holmes weapon.

A blast from it struck the door. It lit up like a Christmas tree for a moment and when the light went away, a steaming hole was made as it passed through six inches of solid steel and concrete.

"Oh, dear God!" Constable Evans uttered.

He ran to the door, pulled on its heavy handle, and then jerked his hand away and let out a harsh yelp of pain.

Watson hurried over to him. "Let me see, Constable."

"Merely a surface burn, nothing to worry about."

Constable Evans scowled at Watson. "Easy for you to say, you don't feel like a boiled lobster."

Watson laughed and then he realized the Constable wasn't laughing and was deadly serious.

He went to the hole in the door and reached a hand out to touch it.

"Not advisable, Watson," Steampunk Holmes commented.

Watson jerked his hand away. He gave them all an alarmed look. "But this is impossible!"

Steampunk stepped closer and cocked his head. "Surely Holmes has told you that when the probable has been examined, we must not..."

"...Rule out the impossible!" Watson finished.

# 221B Baker Street

Mrs. Hudson gently wrapped Constable Evans hand with a large tourniquet, while Watson poured generous doses of vinegar into the cloth.

Watson had done a quick protective wrap at the Yard, but when Constable Evans insisted on going back with them, he had used the opportunity to do a better job on the Constable's burnt hand.

"This is going to hurt a bit, Constable," Watson warned.

Constable Evans clenched his teeth tight but nodded to go ahead.

Watson cinched the tourniquet tight, allowing the fluid to contact the Constable's burnt flesh.

"Damn!" Cursed Constable Evans.

Watson gave him a guilty look.

Steampunk Holmes, smoking a huge cigar, got up from his chair by the fireplace and put a hand on the young man's right shoulder. "Pain can be a fine way to create fortitude in a man's soul, Constable."

"I'd rather not do it that way, if you please, Sherlock."

Steampunk Holmes chuckled.

"Who would?"

Watson sighed. He was having a challenging time adjusting to the new Holmes, and his cavalier attitude towards death and pain. That pressed his mind back into the past once more, remembering the times that Holmes, his Holmes, had spoken about his time in India

Watson felt his heart start to pain him again. He clasped at his heart and groaned lightly.

Steampunk Holmes grabbed him before he could fall, his face filled with alarm and worry.

"Watson!"

"I'm okay; I just need to rest is all."

Challenger and Harry stopped playing chess a moment, equally as alarmed. Conan got up from his chair by the fireplace, ready to administer medical help.

"But you were about to collapse!"

"I'm a doctor, you fool!" Watson snapped and broke free from Steampunk Holmes and wobbled from the room. Mrs. Hudson gave Steampunk a soothing look. "He didn't mean that Sherlock. Please forgive him. He's in a lot of pain and regret right now."

Steampunk nodded. His heart hurt deeply at that time and not just from rejection. He gave her a grateful look before she turned to follow Watson into his room.

Steampunk sat down at the table. Harry and

Challenger was returning to their chess game. "What is that you are playing?"

"It's called chess," Challenger replied. "It's like a battle, but of minds, rather than physical prowess."

Steampunk sat down next to Harry and watched them play about six moves.

Conan sat by the window, reading a paper in the light of a Tesla lamp that overhung that area of the room.

"The weather is supposed to get foul tomorrow," Conan announced.

"It already is," Challenger snorted. "Check!" He said to Harry, who reached for his Bishop.

Steampunk grabbed his hand. "Use your knight!"

Harry glanced at Steampunk. "But you don't even know how to play this game, Sherlock!"

"I do now. Use your knight!"

Challenger laughed. "Go ahead, Harry, I've got the game in three moves anyway. Let the fool prove just how quick he is to judge our skills."

Harry shrugged and did what he been told to do.

When the third move came up, Harry suddenly froze. He eyed his pawn which now blocked Challenger's king from moving, as now the pawn was backed by Harry's bishop, certain to strike Challenger's King if the King moved.

"Checkmate!" Harry cried out triumphantly.

Challenger and Harry, at the same time, turned to eye Steampunk, who only nodded, as he chomped on his cigar and blew out a few large puffy circles of smoke and then poked them with a finger.

"How did you know that?" Conan asked. The very question the other two men were thinking.

"Elementary, Conan," Steampunk explained.

He tapped his head. "Perfect Memory. I can see the moves from the beginning to the end as many as fifty moves ahead."

"Why not more?" Challenger asked in surprise.

"No one's ever lasted longer against me," Steampunk announced. "So, no need," he said with a grin.

"But you said, you never played the game before," Challenger roared, thinking the man had been lying to them all this time.

"I haven't. But as you two played, I was already five games ahead of you and remembering all possible moves." He tapped his head. "It took me one move to understand the players on the board and once I deducted which ones moved in what way by several of your moves, then by the fifth I knew exactly how to win the game and...play it," he answered.

"Now if you'll excuse me, it's been a long day. Good night, my friends," he told them, nodding to all and then he headed for the late Holmes room.

"If Holmes came back now, he'd be in heaven," Conan said with a lilt to his voice. "This man would be a true challenge to him."

Challenger snorted. "If Holmes came back now and found that man in his bed, he would be more than in heaven, good Conan."

The three men laughed, and then they began remembering that their friend was gone, and the weeks were ticking by. Where had he gone? Was he still alive?

And suddenly the warmth of the fireplace had turned cold to them. The lights dim. And once more they felt helpless and lost without their friend.

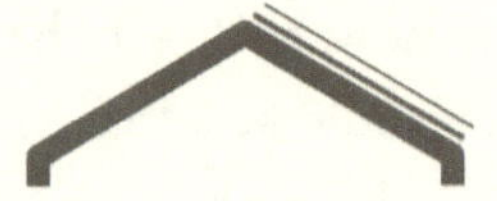

# Watson, Dear Watson I Presume

The soldier, who had cut into the woods after the rest of them had returned to their barracks, was on his knees, peering at the men as they made their way back.

His eyes seemed weary as if a heavy cloud were upon his soul.

"Don't move or you're a dead man!"

The soldier froze. He didn't even blink.

He heard the rustling of leaves behind him and the sound of at least five men walking as quietly as possible to his position.

"Raise your hands and rise slowly!"

He did so.

He started to turn around. Something about the voice sounded familiar to him.

"You so much as move an inch and you will never see your barracks again, soldier. Not that you will anyway, but at least you'll live to regret this day," the voice explained.

Then a pair of hands began unlatching his armor, causing it to fall away from him. As it did so it began to pile around his feet.

The last things to tumble were his weapons.

"Now turn around. Slowly. Very, very slowly."

He turned about slowly. Very, very slowly as asked.

Standing in front of him was a man several inches shorter than him wearing an outfit more fit for the city than combat. He clutched a brown bag in his left hand and a bizarre looking pistol in his right.

"Watson!" He exclaimed, as his mind finally put together all the differing elements of who he was looking at.

"But what are you doing here? This isn't even London," Holmes pointed out.

The man Holmes had identified as Watson didn't speak further, he just gestured with his weapon. "I'll do the questions here, soldier! Now keep those hands up, or I will shoot!"

# 221B Baker Street

You'd think these friends had been up all night as the morning light beat through the Baker Street window, and you'd be right. The coffee pot had been taken and filled again at least a dozen times and replaced.

Mrs. Hudson was still bright and chipper as she came up the stairs with Watson helping her with several trays, loaded with breakfast sandwiches, sliced apples and oranges, and butter.

"Breakfast is served," Mrs. Hudson announced as they entered.

"Did I hear breakfast?" Steampunk Holmes demanded as he stepped into the room also.

Watson glared at the man a moment, then again upon the hurt look returned, he softened. Regret tore at the edges of his heart. "You need to eat just like the rest of us, I presume?" He asked in a somewhat conciliatory tone.

"Do I ever, old chap?" Steampunk Holmes agreed, feeling some sense of acceptance from Watson, however slight softened the blow of the man's brutal responses to him.

Harry and Conan came over from their chairs by the fireplace, where it had burned to embers, which still glowed softly, but not as warmly.

Challenger struggled up from his own chair that had a basket of knitting tools and thread beside it. The one that Mrs. Hudson normally sat upon. He rubbed his eyes. "I could eat a lion."

Watson gave him a surprised look.

Challenger shrugged. "When you have to survive in the jungle, anything not human looks good when you're starving."

Watson didn't give it a response except to roll his eyes. He knew that Challenger had a tendency to exaggerate greatly, though not always, which meant you had to learn to sift out the stretched truths from the reliable, more solid ones.

They all sat together at the table, sharing around the food and drink, then Harry set his coffee cup down after a long gulp from.

"Sherlock."

"Yes, my good man," Steamboat replied.

"Please, Harry."

Steamboat smiled happily. "Indeed, Harry it is!"

Harry leaned forward. "You said that the weapons you use fire a super flux steam of some kind."

"Yes, the steam is focused sort of like those odd little things I've heard some of your people use to send beams of light."

"But steam, by its nature, will vanish once it is released and cools. How do you manage to keep the steam so powerfully tight?"

Steampunk frowned a moment in thought while his hands deftly sliced a piece of his sandwich like a surgeon performing intricate surgery. He looked up. "I suppose its magic of some kind."

"But you said your world doesn't have magic," Harry reminded him.

"Yes, I did. And that's true. The world does not; but the scientists do, and the Goddess does."

But as soon as he mentioned the word Goddess, his smile vanished, and he got a glum look and set the sandwich down he had started to eat and shoved away his plate.

Not lost to the eyes of anyone there. This man was under remarkably close scrutiny for many reasons; the least of them being as to how much they could trust him. Even though he appeared like Sherlock, he might not truly be like him in the best sense of the word.

Harry considered that a long time, nodded and went back to sipping more coffee.

Watson set his cup down and wagged his fork at Steampunk. "So, magic does work there then?"

"Watson, I won't lie to you."

"I should hope not."

Steampunk frowned. "It works there; but only a few can command control of it. The Born!"

"Born?" Watson and Harry asked at the same time.

"You know, from birth. What does that scientist named Barwin call it...ah yes, selective genetic makeup."

"Then magic is not a learned skill on your world?" Challenger asked, perplexed by the answer Steampunk had given.

"No, it is strictly a matter of genetic makeup. A man is always born with it." He paused a long moment, then added, "Or not!"

Mrs. Hudson's face lit up a moment. "Are you saying that women don't have this...this ability?"

Steampunk gave her a kind smile. "I am sorry, my dear heart, but they do not. But if they did, I'm sure you would be the first to have such."

Then his face clouded over again. "But I should add that there is one woman who does have such powers. She is beautiful in every sense of the word and unique in every way. She is like sunshine distilled from rainwater."

Mrs. Hudson smiled. "You sound like a man in love, Sherlock."

"I was."

"Was?"

His face turned dark with anger and regret. "She turned away from the goodness that was given to her at birth and twisted it into something dark and forbidden."

"Who is she?" Watson asked, already knowing what the answer might be.

"The Goddess."

Challenger interrupted the sudden silence by saying. "So therefore, your weapons would not work if handled by a woman then?"

"Not on our world. On yours?" Steampunk replied, and then shrugged.

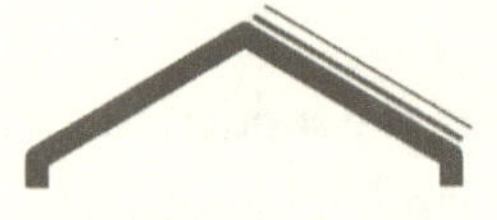

# The Intrigue Deepens

The man was lean and wiry looking, with a thick handlebar mustache, and long sideburns. His hair looked unkempt, but so did that of the other men with him. They all looked weary, beat and highly nervous.

"Holmes!" Watson exclaimed, lowering his weapon at once, and then just as suddenly raising it again.

"Is this some kind of God-awful trick by the Goddess?" Watson demanded, his eyes narrowing in anger, his mustache shaking from the effort to control his emotions.

"Believe me, Watson, I am as surprised to see you as you I," Holmes replied, the hint of a smile on his lips.

"But you are so...so...young!" Watson pointed out, the look of skepticism on his face not going away.

Holmes smiled, "And you...not by much."

Watson actually smiled a moment. "By ten years at the least, I suspect."

He lowered his weapon again and nodded to the others. They all lowered their weapons and dispersed back into the shrubs of the woods, leaving Watson and Holmes together alone.

Watson sat down on a fallen tree trunk and crossed one leg over the other. "It saddens me to see you."

"It gladdens me to see you," Holmes replied. Then he smirked. "Even if a tad older."

Watson laughed again. He wiped at his eyes, which were beginning to tear up. "I thought…"

He looked at the weapon in his hands, and then put it back into its holster beneath his right armpit. The glow of its barrels clicked off.

He looked back at Holmes.

"This is impossible, you know."

Holmes nodded. "But…"

"When the possible becomes improbable…"

"The impossible must be considered," Holmes finished for Watson.

Watson reached a hand out. "We have much to talk about."

Holmes took the hand and shook it firmly. "Much indeed!"

The sound of shouts broke the falling night air.

Watson jumped up. He cupped a hand to his ear to listen.

More shouting.

He glanced at Holmes. "We must leave here. They must have found the ships."

"Found what?" Holmes replied, as he followed Watson deeper into the woods.

"We sabotaged a squadron of their attack craft."

Watson stopped a moment to look into Holmes face. "You're not from this world, are you?"

"Your ability to make a reasonable deduction is remarkable, Watson. But then, you're not from this one either, are you?"

Watson smiled.

# The Goddess

She sat before an antique mirror, its wood frame clutching the mirror glass with tiny spider like hands that ended in gold shells. The desk the mirror sat upon had been constructed from a deep, dark, and highly polished wood with patterns of leaves and flowers embedded into it. The drawers had latches made from gear handles and the wood faces had the hint of shadowy forms in its lustrous veneer.

She sighed.

The pale mask she always wore to hide her true identity and face fell away into her lap. She gently lifted it and placed it upon the desk before the mirror. She gazed at the horrible white face she had concocted to put terror into those who gazed upon her and smiled.

She raised her hair brush, which had tiny hands about its edges that clasped glowing crystals and began brushing her long, long hair. She always had to bury it inside the mask, but the cloak and hood hid it so well, she never worried about a stray strand showing. She had planned perfectly for just such a thing.

She sighed.

Being a cruel woman wasn't in her nature from birth. It was an acquired taste. Only one man had seen through the mask she wore, and she still resented him for it; despised him for it; loved him for it.

She gazed at the liquid beauty of her face. She was still so young. The years did not accent her forehead with wrinkles, or her cheeks with marks of ageing. Why? She wasn't sure. Something different in her physical makeup.

But her brains. There, she had always been exceptionally bright, and her father had been a genius. So not a major surprise when some of that rubbed off on her.

The youthfulness was a mystery to her and something that allowed her to keep her people enthralled by the mystery of her. After all, she'd outlived so many of them.

The real surprise was when she turned her intellect not to building up the Empire of her world, but to subjugating it. When she was smaller, she was terrified of the boys. She still remembered that wintry night when a group of them had crept into her bedroom when her father was gone, away on one of his many missions of mercy to help the poor and downtrodden.

She despised him for being gone. Hated him for it. Hated the ones he had helped at the cost of her innocence.

For it meant her youth, her innocence was as lost to her as a cob of corn has its husk stripped away to reveal the tender meat inside. But in her case, it was a brutal and unforgiving rape.

She had spent over ten hours in surgery when her father found her lying on the floor of her bedroom, sobbing in pain, bleeding on the floor, unable to move. He had gently lifted her up and run with her to the nearest hospital. No cabs out that late at night. He had run through dark alleys and once even fought off a mugger who was stupid enough to get into his way. The man died there. No loss to her or the father, she thought as a reflection.

It had taken the surgeons hours to reconstruct her feminine area. Bones were broken and separated. Blood vessels forever lost. It was a miracle she didn't die from the bleeding, let alone from the damage to her internal organs. But somehow, they reconstructed her bit by bit.

Maybe it was then that something had changed in her body chemistry. She vaguely remembered one of the doctors as being someone who shouldn't have been there. He stood in the background, watching her intently and leaned upon a strong staff that had a slight cast of greenish gold to it.

Before she had sunk into anesthesia yet again, the pain had caused her to surface into consciousness again; he had actually smiled, nodded his head and then vanished.

That was the last she had seen of him and even now trying to remember him clearly caused her head to hurt; so, she stopped, even as she had been doing for years now. Haunted by a stranger and a memory she couldn't understand the significance of.

She sighed and glanced at her lap whch was covered with her makeup cloth and her robe beneath that.

She never looked at that part of her body anymore. It was so heavy with scarring it caused her nightmares. But she did allow others to look, her handmaidens. They understood at once when they saw it.

None ever complained in helping her. This was good, as she would not have allowed them to serve her otherwise, or live! She was not cruel; she just couldn't allow others to know of her weakness, her vulnerability.

And she began to sob briefly. He had seen it. He had seen it and yet had said nothing. Had loved her all the more because of it. She hated him for that. Even the memory of his hand gently pressing against her there stung sharply, even as at the time it had brought her a sense of relief and self-rejuvenation she had never experienced before.

*Where are you?* She thought briefly. Her lack of attention and sudden anger and despair caused her to lose focus on her right hand, which had been clasping a perfume bottle, suddenly crushed it, causing it to shatter into dozens of pieces and douse her and her robe with the liquid of the perfume.

The pain of the cuts was extreme; but it matched what she felt inside as well. Now she could hold it back no longer. She could hold it within no more.

She threw her head into her arms and began sobbing. Over and over and over.

And as long as she stayed in her Inner Sanctum none would ever know that the Goddess had a heart like them!

# 221B Baker Street Alternate World

"This way, Holmes," Watson said as he worked his way up a series of stairs that had odd mechanical gear shapes embossed on their railing and steps shaped like mirrors, but with no reflection.

"Very creative," Holmes said.

"What?" Watson glanced where Holmes was looking. "Oh that, very modest as stairs go."

Holmes arched an eyebrow.

Watson laughed. "Haven't seen that look in a while. It's nice to see it again, even though..."

Watson lapsed into silence, shook his head, and then began ascending again.

"What address is this, Watson?"

"I imagine not much different than your own worlds, 221B Baker Street."

Holmes nodded.

Watson stopped on a landing.

A matronly woman opened a door several doorways down and peeked out. "John, must you be so noisy when you come home? And who's this stranger?"

Watson waved at her, then said, "Dear Mrs. Hudson, can't you recognize my old friend? It's Sherlock. Sherlock Holmes."

She strained her eyes to look at him. "Looks different."

She came a bit closer to examine Holmes more carefully. "You been going to those Paris salons, Mister Holmes, you look younger, fresher."

"I don't feel that way," Holmes replied.

She reached out and pinched his bottom.

"Do to me!" She cackled, then went back to her door, entered, and closed it.

"Cheerful sort, but a bit on the...ummm...vulgar side," Watson declared.

Holmes nodded. He had been so shocked by the action of the woman that he hadn't considered that not only would the woman look a bit different than his own Mrs. Hudson, but that she might be different as well!

Watson smiled, seeing the look on Holmes face. "You'll get used it, she's really quite likable, if you ignore the occasional pinch of affection."

He opened the first door on his right and swung it inwards. "Here we are."

Holmes went inside and reached for the electric switch but grabbed something else that screeched instead. He hurriedly withdrew his hand.

Watson came inside laughing. "Sorry, old chap. I should have warned you. Polly likes to perch on the wall there.

He clapped his hands, and a burst of steam brushed his and Holmes faces, then lights slowly began coming up about the room.

Polly was a cute cockatiel. It was perched on a unique ornament that was shaped like a hand poking from the wall and had eight fingers, all extra-long, and each one holding a hat, an umbrella, or a coat.

Polly cocked his head and eyed Holmes thoughtfully, "Pretty boy!"

Holmes laughed.

Watson watched him a moment, then nodded, as if having decided something.

Holmes didn't notice, Polly had decided to hop onto his shoulder and nuzzle his right ear.

"Does she do this all the time?"

"He, Sherlock, he. Don't insult him or he might bite you instead."

Holmes smiled and took the bird carefully from his shoulder and put him back on his prior perch.

Polly ruffled up and said, "Pretty Boy!"

Holmes turned to look into the room he had been brought into. It was stunning. Every single thing he was used to seeing at his own home was here, but with modifications. There were gears molded into every piece of furniture, clocks, and pipes and so little of it seemed to have a visible function.

Watson laughed again. "Don't be alarmed, you'll get used to it. Babies do."

Holmes turned to Watson. "I'm not a baby."

"I know, so it should be even easier, I imagine."

Holmes had no argument for that logic, so he said nothing. He allowed his right hand to glide across the top of the sofa set before the fireplace and all the myriad gadgets embedded to its top and back were amazing.

"Do any of these actually have a function, Watson?"

"Oh, most do. It takes time to acquaint oneself to them though. Even a grown man has problems at times figuring which one does what, when there's so many of the newfangled things to work with." He said in disgust.

Inventors on our world are going crazy

making all these gadgets and adding them to common everyday devices, furniture, and clothing. Myself, I would love to go back to the old days, when a coat was just a coat. But I will admit," he said, patting the holster beneath his coat and the devices beneath the holster that glowed there, "I will admit that sometimes the devices can be life savers."

Holmes arched an eyebrow. "You disapprove?"

"No," Watson sighed. "It's just that one has to spend so much time cleaning and polishing to keep everything nice. Whoever began inventing all this rubbish was obviously not a woman."

Holmes arched his eyebrows even more. "Not a woman?"

Watson turned to face his new found friend. "Oh, right, you're not from here, are you? It's this way, Holmes; women here are the ones running the show these days. Men have to tread lightly, or they can end up on the streets without a job."

Holmes sat down in a highly polished wooden chair draped by a blanket of gear like colored threads emblazoned on it. He felt the texture a moment, and then looked up as Watson stood before the fire watching him silently. "It looks hard to the eyes but is soft to the touch."

Watson chuckled. "You are like Mrs. Hudson's child next door; everything is fresh and new to you."

Holmes nodded. And then he gave Watson a double take. "That...was Mrs. Hudson?"

He remembered Watson saying so, but still found it hard to match this woman with the one that his Watson loved.

"Aye, it was. A bit on the plump side, but a good soul. Her husband does a decent job of taking care of the house."

Holmes smiled. This world was turning out to be stranger than he had at first thought. She had a husband. Was overweight. And Watson here on this world was trim and healthy as an ox. Strange indeed.

Then Holmes was shocked further when a mechanical being shaped like a woman rolled into the room with clocks for eyes and a grid across her chest, with a mop in one hand and a broom in the other. "Master Watson, I have finished scouring the floors, sweeping the bathroom, and washing the dishes. Will there be anything else before I turn off for the night to recharge?"

"No, Tilda, thank you so much."

"You're very welcome, Master Watson," she said, then she rolled into a corner near the window and lights lit up about her waist, elbows and feet all went dark.

"Handy little thing!" Holmes said admiringly.

Watson grinned. "I made her."

Now Holmes almost jumped out of his seat at that news. "That's remarkable. Very, very remarkable."

"What Tilda? Nah., I built her in my spare time at the shop with Jules and Wells. They have a tiny engineering shop down the street. Edison and Tesla are their rivals and they hired me to act as a go-between."

"Go between?"

Watson patted his weapon. "To make sure they didn't get between us and our work."

"Then they're villains here?"

Watson frowned. "They're not on your world?"

Holmes shook his head.

"I see," Watson said. "Well, here, they're not so much villains as pains in the arse. They still ideas and market them as their own."

"But they're geniuses!" Holmes exclaimed.

"Not here," Watson explained. "Here they're just trolls out to make a quick buck, sort of like those two scoundrels from America, B and T."

"B and T?"

Watson sighed. "You really are from a different world, aren't you?" Watson asked. He sat down and motioned for Holmes to sit down next to him.

"If you're going to survive here, you need to understand things a bit more."

"Watson, just one question overwhelming demands my attention at this moment."

And it is?"

"When do you have time to do your medical practice?"

Watson's happy face vanished.

# At a Glance

The two men stole stealthily through the alley, dodging discarded trash and containers, small puddles of murky water, keeping to the shadows as a constable stood with his back to the alley, watching a woman and her child walk past.

"Good evening, Missus Yorkshire!" The constable greeted.

"Good evening, Constable Faraday," She greeted back. She stopped a moment.

"Harold, isn't there something you want to say too?"

Harold, about three years old, screwed his mouth up in a contortion to speak and spoke. "Papa!"

Constable Faraday burst into laughter.

Harold reached his hands out, hopefully.

Constable Faraday grabbed him up and swung him in circles to the child's delight. Harold screamed and screamed, but all happy screams.

Finally, Constable Faraday set the child down and Missus Yorkshire took his hand again. "You are so good with children, Constable Faraday."

He tipped his hat to her. "I could be even better to their mother, I imagine," he said boldly.

She put a hand to her mouth and laughed.

Then she screamed. "Look out!"

The Constable swung around, grabbing for his nightstick, but the two men were faster. They fired their odd weapons, striking him fully in the chest. He burst into flames and collapsed to the ground, a horrified look on his face.

Harold began screaming with terror.

Missus Faraday swung her child up into her arms and made to run off, but the two men intercepted her. "Don't harm my child!" She begged.

Harold reached out a hand and punched the nearest of the men on his nose.

The man's face darkened, and his teeth clenched in anger.

"Please," she begged, seeing the look on his face.

He smiled, but his smile gave no sense of relief as he reached out.

"I wouldn't if I were you, Old Chap," Steampunk Holmes stated.

The two men swung around.

Steampunk had a weapon in both hands and aimed at their chests. "What goes around as they say."

The larger of the two men rushed Steampunk, who merely stepped to the side and swatted him to the ground with the butt of his weapon, while keeping the other trained on the remaining man.

"Now then," Steampunk Holmes began. "Shall we take a little stroll? I hear that the evening airs here are quite good for the constitution. And the cells of Scotland Yard are hungry for new occupants."

Missus Faraday wiped at the tears in her eyes as she turned away from the sight of the one, she had loved, whose body was now just ashes on the pavement.

"Who are you, sir? I feel, I and my child owe you a word of thank...thanks..."

She tried to be brave, but her heart hurt too much to keep up that lie. She burst into tears.

Steampunk's eyes narrowed.

The other man chose that moment to try and make a break for it.

Steampunk tripped him and clobbered him

on his head, sending him into darkness.

He rose and went to Missus Faraday, "You're safe now, Madam."

She shook her head. "I'll never feel safe again now!" She wept, her eyes on the man she had loved.

Steampunk's face, for the first time we've known him, appears stricken by what he sees and hears. Some of the false braggadocio he was showing melts away as he reaches out and gently enfolds her in his arms, absorbing her sadness into his chest and wondering why he was sent to such a hellish place, but at the same time wondering if it was really so different from his own world.

And if it was...very much the same..., why was he feeling so much more now than on his own world?

These were questions that plagued his heart at that moment, sundering his invisible shield of self-protection from his own sense of vulnerability that he had been safely building up over the years, and was now opening up and threatening to engulf him in a tidal wave of new feelings.

Harold, who had been screaming over and over between he and the woman, became quieter as his mother cried and Steampunk refused to let them go, for some reason that he couldn't explain.

# Scotland Yard

"There must be some kind of pattern to this dratted business of killing our people," Inspector Bloodstone shouted at his men and women in the staff room.

They all had glum faces, and many had been weeping. Inspector Bloodstone stiffened a moment in anger, and then at a look from his son, Constable Evans, he relented.

"I'm sorry; it's not like we're not all doing our bloody best. But there has to be a pattern to this all!" He reiterated.

"There is!" Steampunk Holmes announced as he stepped into the building and tossed the two men from the alley to the floor in the center of the room onto the table there.

Gasps. Looks of disbelief.

"Holmes!" The Inspector gasped. "What's the meaning of this?"

Steampunk brightened. "Why thank you, Inspector a rather unexpected sound of encouragement from you."

Constable Evans whispered in his father's right ear.

"Oh that!" The Inspector said, sniffling slightly. "It's easier to say than...than..."

"Steampunk, father."

"Steampunk father," the Inspector repeated. "I mean Steampunk!" He quickly corrected himself, blushing at his mistake.

Steampunk plunked a hand on the Inspector's shoulder.

Everyone in the room tensed, waiting for the Inspector to burst into one of his invectives or at the very least shove the man's hand away.

It didn't happen; he actually stood there, accepting the act as a kind of act of friendship, even though he thoroughly detested the man.

"You said?"

"What I said," Steampunk began, "Is that I know the pattern, because it's the same one I fought in my own world."

"Which is?"

"The Goddess."

The Inspector waved to his people. "Out, out! Get busy and make your lives useful!" He ordered.

Everyone left, but many were smiling or laughing.

The Inspector made a growling sound deep in his throat and the rest hurried out silently and as quickly as they could, leaving just the Inspector, his son and Steampunk in the room.

"That person again?"

Steampunk sat down between the two unconscious men and rested a metal gloved hand on each one's back. He tapped his right-hand index finger over and over on that man's head as if waiting for a hollow sound to occur. "Well, it makes sense to me. You don't need to be a Steampunk Wizard to know the color of the sky is blue, you know."

The Inspector gave him a blank stare.

Steampunk sighed. He got back up, but as one of the men stirred, he smashed his head with a gloved hand, sending him back into unconsciousness. "The Goddess has only one goal in her life; however short or miserably long it might be. And from what I've heard and been able to research...or was able to know that I'm here...is that she's been around much longer than normal. Hence, her anointed with the title of Goddess.

"You saying she's immortal like those dratted Elves?"

"Elves?" Steampunk asked, his face blank.

The Inspector sighed. "Never mind. Later,"

Steampunk cocked his head as if considering what the Inspector had blurted out. Finally, he got back on track and said, "Let's just say that her goal is to make the world a worse place than it started off. She hates all the worlds and especially ones where men are in power."

"Such as ours?" The Inspector asked.

Steampunk nodded.

"But why?" The Inspector demanded. "Why does she hate men so much? It's irrational!"

Steampunk's face clouded over for a moment as he remembered something he had wished to bury and then said, "She has her reasons."

"Any rate," the Inspector went on. "We're creating equality with women all the time now. Soon there will be no differences..."

The Inspector blushed. "Well, some will remain, but you know..."

Steampunk smiled. "Oh, I do. I do!"

He slapped the Inspector on his back, "And thank the Creator for there are!"

The Inspector scowled at the hand still on his back and Steampunk hurriedly removed it.

The Inspector backed up out of Steampunk's reach.

"Yes," the Inspector agreed. Sort of. But something was not revealed. He frowned.

Constable Evans spoke up for his flustered father. "I get the sense there's something more you're not telling us about this...evil woman, this Goddess?

Steampunk suddenly looked distant and sad. "Not all evil starts out that way," he said, and then his eyes seemed to water slightly. He rubbed at them.

"Something got in my eyes,"

"Anyway, fix them up in a nice uncomfortable cell, will you?"

He left the room hurriedly.

# 221B Baker Street

Watson sat down at the table and faced Harry. Challenger and Conan sat by the fire reading the London Times Evening Edition, pretending not to listen to what was being said.

Mrs. Hudson sat in her rocking chair, a worried look creasing her brow, but saying nothing, knitting a small towel with bright colored red roses on its edges.

"We've spent weeks now scouring for Holmes and still no word of him, Harry," Watson complained, a sense of utter disappointment in his eyes and on his face.

"We'll find him, Watson," Harry uttered. "I swear we will!"

Watson sighed and put a hand on Harry's right arm. "I know you're doing your best, Harry. We all are. It's just..."

Harry put his hand over Watson's and squeezed it warmly. "I know. I know."

"Holmes!"

Nothing more needed to be said. It weighed equally as heavy on all their hearts, tugging at them, pricking them, tearing them slowly apart a bit at a time. No one can be that close to another and not feel the pain of separation. Missing them. Walking into a room they once were, but it's now empty.

Only memories left.

And those fading away as well with time.

# Warehouse Nine

Commander Richards stood before his assembled troops. None of them were in uniform. About twenty all together stood before him.

"We have a problem."

The men muttered amongst themselves a moment in agreement.

Some of them turned to the side and glanced at the prisoners they had been accumulating. There were men and women, all sealed into tall glass capsules covered with strange machinery and readouts. They were all stark naked and bathed in a garish red light that strobe and pass up their bodies, then down, and then up again and so forth over and over.

"We have accumulated a few recruits, but we need more and now the city is on to us," Commander Richards said.

What he didn't say was that the Goddess, who had made him commander, would not be very happy that their mission was running into difficulty on this backward world and not only that but that the very man she hated with all her being was behind much of the problems they were running into.

A burst of energy lit up a huge ring of cylinders and they began moving in all manner of directions, some sideways, some upside down, or to the left or right. Dials began humming with activity on the consoles built into the rings.

Several men monitoring the huge device stepped back as a form began to take shape in front of the cylinders and gears, then take shape, at first vaguely feminine, then a form wearing a heavy cloak of burnished gold and shirt and pants of heavy gear symbols stepped through the shape.

The men in the room went to full attention as the Commander stepped to greet her.

He half bowed to her and then said, "Goddess!"

# 221B Baker Street Alternate World

Holmes sat in a chair overlooking Baker Street. It was as different from his world's street as night was from day. Instead of the smooth, slick looking Tesla cars with their glowing electric engines mounted on their hoods, the cars here had smokestack like pipes that rose from the front, back or sides, emitting puffs of steam in rhythm to the internal engines, safely hidden beneath huge, hooded covers in front.

Even the wheels of the cars were unique, with the front ones smaller than the rear ones, so that the back of the cards protruded upwards, giving the cars an almost cat like stance, ready to pounce in appearance.

A heavy whirring sound caught his attention, and he looked up just as a strange bicycle with two cigar shaped balloons holding it up in the air, flew past, small propellers driven by the action of the men's feet on the pedals of the bike.

Then a horn honking drew his attention to a huge truck shaped like a box with wooden sides, huge windows and passengers seated inside reading newspapers. Smoke stacks puffed steam from the room and the driver sat on a raised seat the front of the box, which was uplifted by a series of interconnected tubes.

The man squeezed a ball next to his steering wheel and a huge horn mounted on both sides of the box shape blasted.

Pedestrians on both sides of Baker Street rushed to get aboard once the bus slowed and pulled to the curb.

Several children skated by on thin wooden skateboards with thrusters and engines that shot hot steam from their nozzles.

"Most interesting," Holmes uttered to himself.

"I imagine our world is quite a shocker compared to your own, Holmes."

Holmes turned from the window to look at Watson, who had shaved and slipped into a bathrobe of brilliant red colors made of some kind of soft material that he called puff. Evidently there were creatures on this planet that were used solely for their...puff...which caused Holmes to smile, since he had various ideas of what they might look like with a name such as theirs was.

"No so much shock, as unique."

Holmes reached to the small table next to him and uncapped a colorful tin with pictures of elephants wearing rocket packs on their sides with huge steam pipes on their rears. He plucked some tobacco from it and placed it the pipe in his left hand. "Your Holmes doesn't smoke pipes, I take it?"

Watson pulled up a chair next to Holmes and shook his head. "Smokes those horrible cigars. Part of the reason we separated. Horrible smell. Horrible on the lungs."

Holmes was halfway to lighting his pipe and hesitated.

Watson smile. "Don't worry; if his cigars haven't killed me, your pipe is much less likely too, old chap. And even if I don't know you personally that well, I know your pattern enough that you probably need that right about now, good fellow."

Holmes returned the smile and lit his pipe. He took several pulls on it, and then blew out a gray haze of purling smoke.

"Time to talk, Watson. You've been quite gracious with your time...and..." Holmes gestured to the tin of tobacco, "But I know something's on your mind. You may be different in some ways, but in others not so much."

"So, you see, Holmes, that we are on an equal footing as to how we perceive each other," Watson agreed.

"You know, Holmes," Watson said with the touch of irony in his voice. "You are much like my own Holmes, but I'd have to say quite a bit less arrogant and bullheaded."

Holmes eyebrows rose questioningly.

Watson sighed, cupped his palms about his right knee and looked out the window at the stars popping into the sky as the night grew darker and lights began darkening about the city.

"When we first met, we were quite young; both determined to make a difference in our world. He through his deductions and I through my..."

Watson had a tough time getting it out, but finally managed, "My medicine."

Watson froze a moment, unable to speak further.

"John, you loved your medicine more than life itself, what happened to you?"

Watson turned to look Holmes square in the eye. "I lost someone quite dear to me."

He suddenly looked extremely angry, hurt, and utterly lost at the same time, rubbing his forehead and bristling mustache as if that would somehow soothe all the emotions he was feeling at that moment. "It stripped the heart right out of me. I gave up on everything. Everything!"

He looked to Holmes, who waited patiently, a look of compassion on his face. "I even ran away from you!"

He smiled faintly. "Not that I didn't have dozens of reasons for doing so; but I would never willingly abandon a friend in need. But he was never one to show that side of him," Watson said sadly.

"Perhaps if he had, then we'd both be in a better space now."

Holmes reached out a hand and put it gently on Watson's hand. "John, I'm sure my double would take you back in the blink of an eye, no matter how different," he said with a smile, "Or difficult he might be. I know us too well!"

Watson laughed and shook his head.

"The man, wherever he is now, is probably laughing, having a good time, bragging about his latest exploits and looking for his latest feminine conquest." Watson said, his voice rich with sadness.

# 221B Baker Street

Steampunk Holmes stood on the front porch of the flat, a cigar burning in his right hand, and a heap of ashes on the pavement that tells us he hasn't touched it to his lips even once.

He has his eyes on the distant stars. His eyes are unfocused as if looking elsewhere, even though the skies are magnificent, crystal-clear and bright with splashes of silver light upon the few clouds hovering above.

Even the moon is full, its luminous face shining brightly upon the city of London.

Not a sound comes from about the man. The street is quiet. No foot or car traffic.

"Watson," he sighs.

While he sighs for what is denied him, there are those above him, watching from the rooftop. Men with glowing boots.

They smile, reach for their weapons, draw them, and point them at the sad figure below.

"For the Goddess!" They both cry out.

Then they fire!

PAGE |

# Don't miss out!

Visit the website below and you can sign up to receive emails whenever John Pirillo publishes a new book. There's no charge and no obligation.

https://books2read.com/r/B-A-EMSD-JOHDC

BOOKS 2 READ

Connecting independent readers to independent writers.

Did you love *Battle for Earth*? Then you should read *Invasion* by John Pirillo!

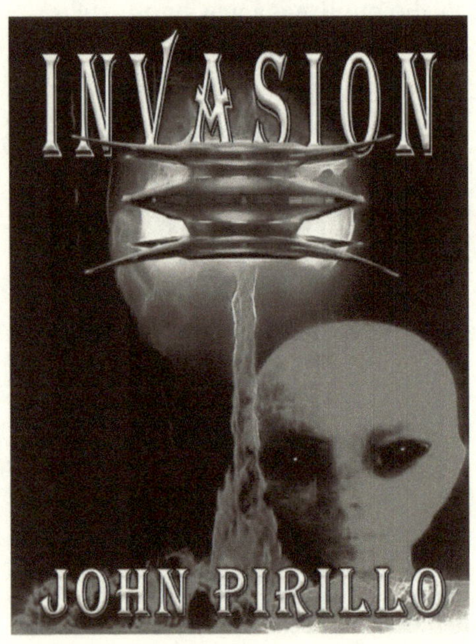

The battleship off the coast of England thought it was the most powerful weapon on the sea.*It was wrong!*Rising from the depths is an intruder.A machine so powerful.So deadly.That the battleship is blown apart in seconds.**The intruder has demonstrated its power and now turns to England.***Soon, it will bring its war to land.Nothing will get in its way.*Jules Verne and H.G. Wells are two young friends with a common ambition...to court young women, and to become famous writers.*But when their fathers are called off to a war no one knows anything about, both young men are about toenter a world of pain and suffering that only the strongest will survive.The Invasion has begun and if the two young men don't do something drastic, they too will become casualties of the war.Realizing their fathers are not going to return from the battle going on, Jules and Wells decide to fight the Invaders.But what*

can these two young men do to stop an invasion...from Mars?Book One of the War of the Worlds.*Buy your book now.*

Read more at www.johnpirillo.com.

# Also by John Pirillo

**Angel Hamilton**
Broken Fangs


**Baker Street Universe Tales**
Baker Street Universe Tales
Baker Street Universe Tales 2
Baker Street Universe Tales 3
Baker Street Universe Tales 4
Baker Street Universe Tales 5
Baker Street Universe Tales Seven


**Between**
Prince of Between


**"Classic Baker Street Universe Sherlock Holmes"**
Sherlock Holme: Hyde's Night of Terror
Case of the Deadly Goddess
Case of the Abominable

## Detective Judge Dee
Detective Dee Murder Most Chaste

## Elektron
Elektron

## Escape To Adventure
Escape to Adventure
Escape to Atlantis

## Hollow Earth Special Forces
Hollow Earth Special Forces, Forbidden World

## Holmes
Sherlock Holmes Struck
Sherlock Holmes A Dangerous Act

## Infinite Tales
Infinite Tales
Infinite Tales Two

**Mystery Knight**
HellBound Mystery
Hell Bound Angel


**PhaseShift**
PhaseShift
PhaseShift Two: Crossover
PhaseShift: Shifting Worlds


**Rocketman**
Rocketman
Rocket Man, Mission Berlin
Rocketman Christmas
Rocket Man, Sky Commando
Time Wars


**Sherlock Holmes**
Sherlock Holmes, ICE
The Ice Man
Sherlock Holmes Fallen
Sherlock Holmes: Monster
Sherlock Holmes: Tick Tock
Sherlock Holmes Christmas Magic
Sherlock Holmes Dark Secret
Sherlock Holmes Shadow of Dorian Gray
Sherlock Holmes Vampire

Sherlock Holmes: Cursed in Stone
Sherlock Holmes Apparition
Sherlock Holmes Case of the Raging Madness
Sherlock Holmes Dark Princess
Sherlock Holmes Dark Angel
Constable Evans' Fancy
Sherlock Holmes Matter of Perception
Sherlock Holmes Tangled
Sherlock Holmes Case of the Gossamer Lady
Sherlock Holmes House of Shadows
Sherlock Holmes The Yellow Death
Sherlock Holmes Oblique
Sherlock Holmes Mystery Train Winter Collection
Sherlock Holmes A Tale Less Told
Sherlock Holmes Mystery Six
Sherlock Holmes, Rules of Darkness, Special Edition
Sherlock Holmes Shape of Justice
Sherlock Holmes Christmas Magic
Sherlock Holmes Fallen Angel
Ghostly Shadows
Sherlock Holmes: Artifact
Sherlock Holmes Bloody Hell
Sherlock Holmes Monster of the Tower
Sherlock Holmes Darkest of Nights
Sherlock Holmes Nightmare
Sherlock Holmes Poetry of Death
Sherlock Holmes, Dracula
Sherlock Holmes #3, Ice Storm


**Sherlock Holmes Urban Fantasy Mysteries**
Sherlock Holmes Urban Fantasy Mysteries 2

Sherlock Holmes Urban Fantasy Mysteries 3
Sherlock Holmes Urban Fantasy Mysteries 4
Sherlock Holmes, The Dracula Files
Sherlock Holmes, Dark Clues
Sherlock Holmes, Case of the Undying Man
Sherlock Holmes, Mystery of the Sea
Sherlock Holmes, Night Watch
Sherlock Holmes, Mystery of the Path not Taken
Sherlock Holmes, the Dorian Gray Affair
The Baker Street Universe
Sherlock Holmes, The Dracula Affair
Baker Street Universe Tales 6
Spector
Sherlock Holmes, Rules of Darkness


**The Baker Street Detective**
Strange Times, The Baker Street Detective, Book2
The Baker Street Detective, Hollow Man
The Baker Street Detective 5, The Howling Wind


**Urban Fantasies**
Urban Fantasies


**War of the Worlds**
Battle for Earth

**Standalone**

Sherlock Holmes Deadly Consequences

Invisibility Factor

Red Painted Souls

Between

Robin Hood

Shadow Man

The Rainbow Bridge

Cartoon, Johnnie Angel

Sherlock Holmes 221B

Sherlock Holmes Shape Shifter

Urban Fantasy Mysteries

Sherlock Holmes, Urban Fantasy Mysteries

Halloween Mysteries

Invasion

Romancing the Word

Romancing the Word Workbook


Watch for more at www.johnpirillo.com.

www.ingramcontent.com/pod-product-compliance
Lightning Source LLC
Chambersburg PA
CBHW051227160726
47994CB00002B/777